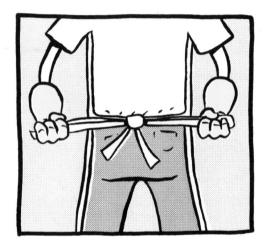

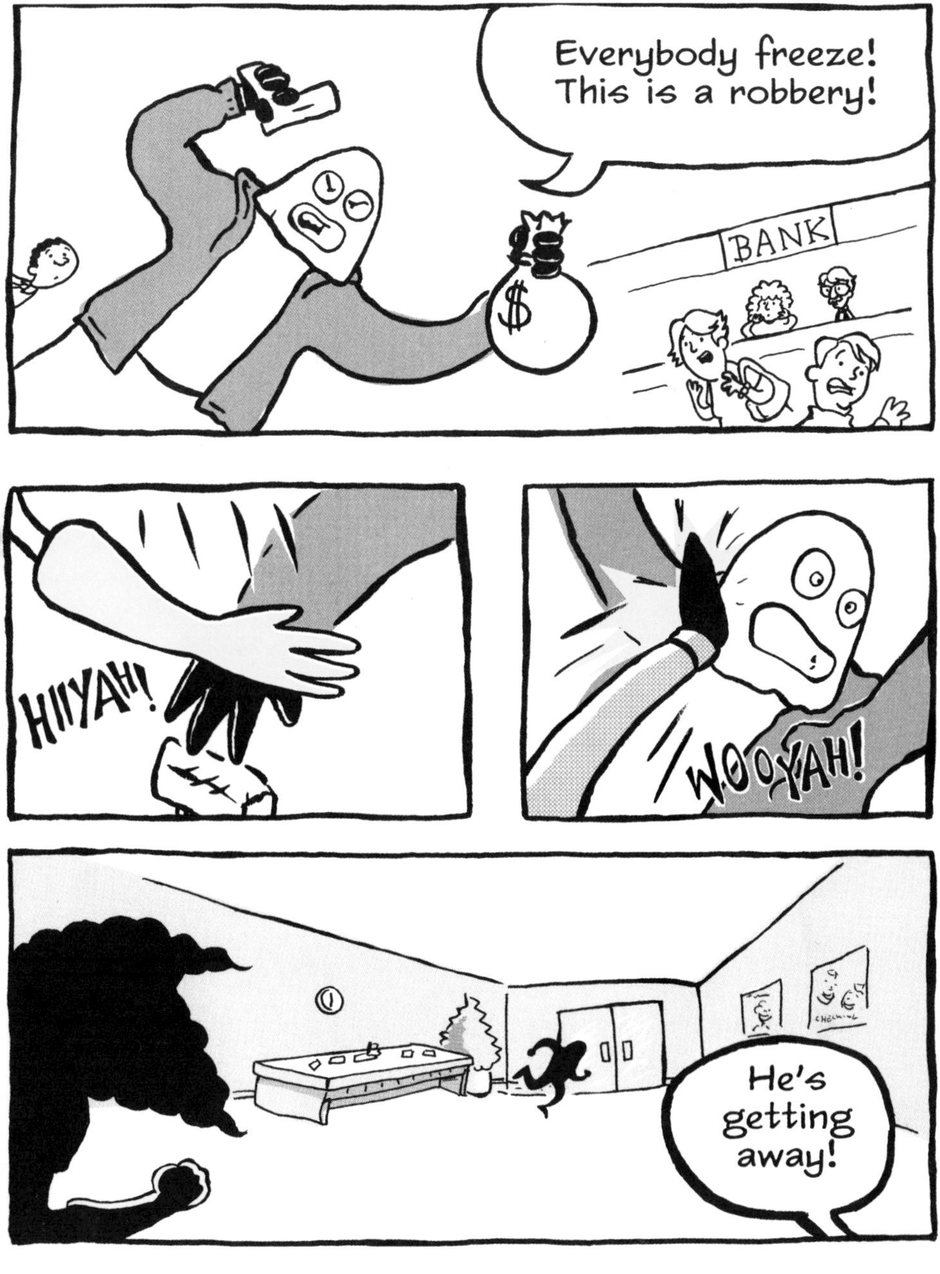
Everybody freeze! This is a robbery!
BANK
HIIYAH!
WOOYAH!
He's getting away!

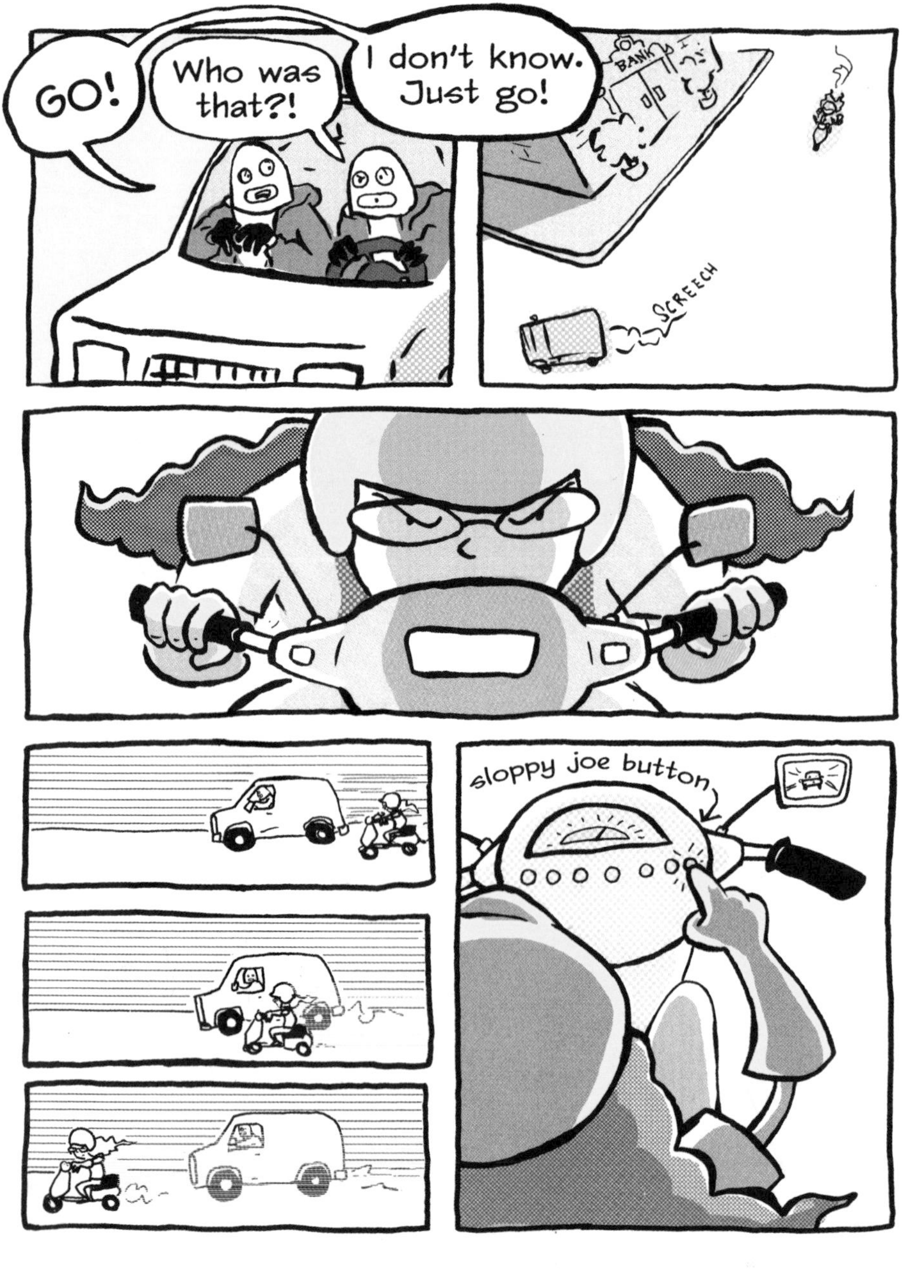
GO!
Who was that?!
I don't know. Just go!
BANK
SCREECH
sloppy joe button

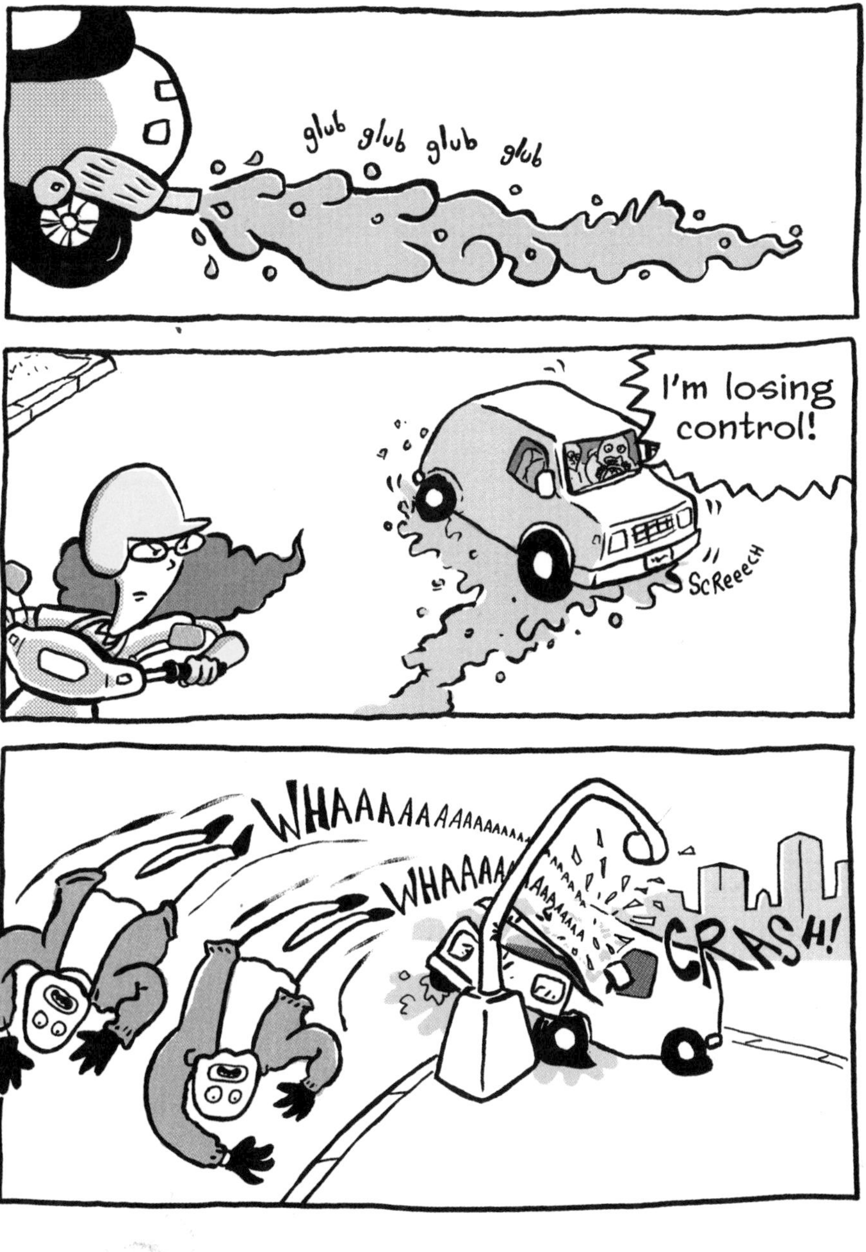
glub glub glub glub
I'm losing control!
SCREEECH
WHAAAAAAAAAAAAAAA
WHAAAAAAAAAAA
CRASH!

LUNCH

Jarrett J. Krosoczka

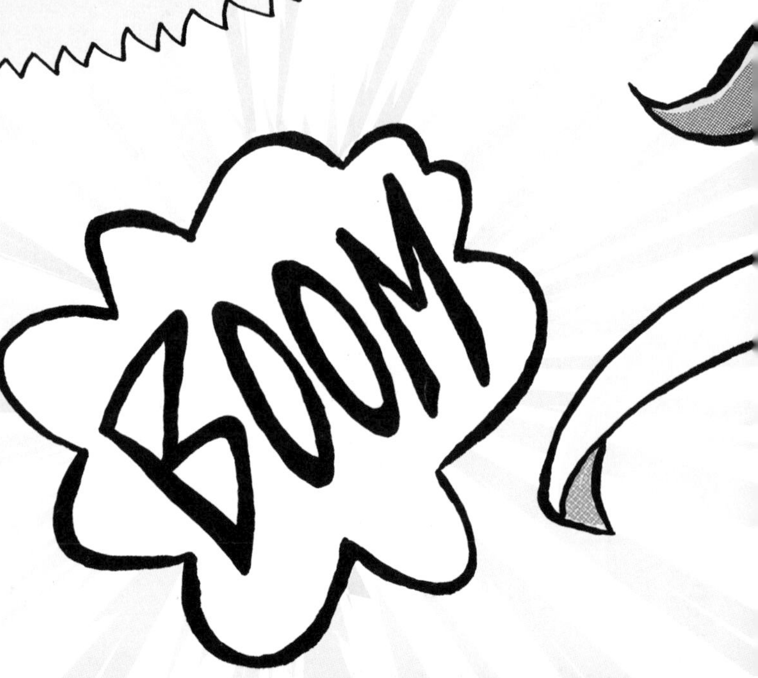
BOOM

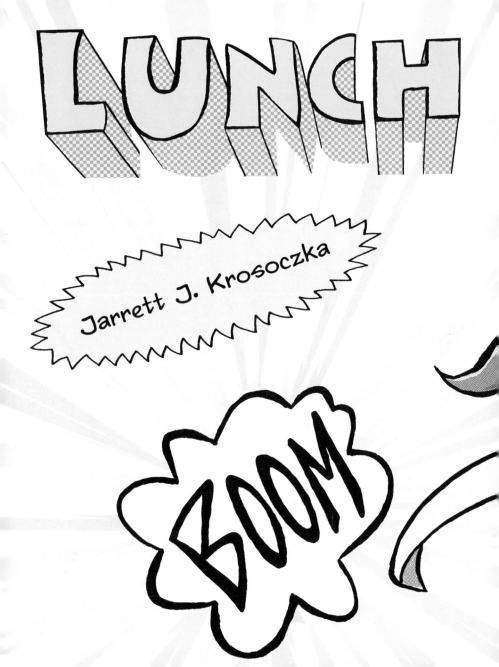

LADY

and the Cyborg Substitute

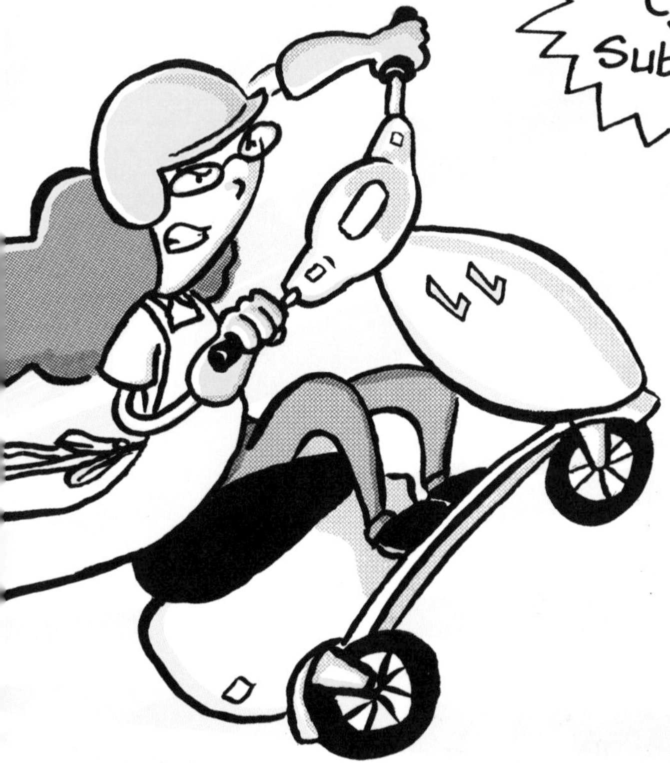

Alfred A. Knopf New York

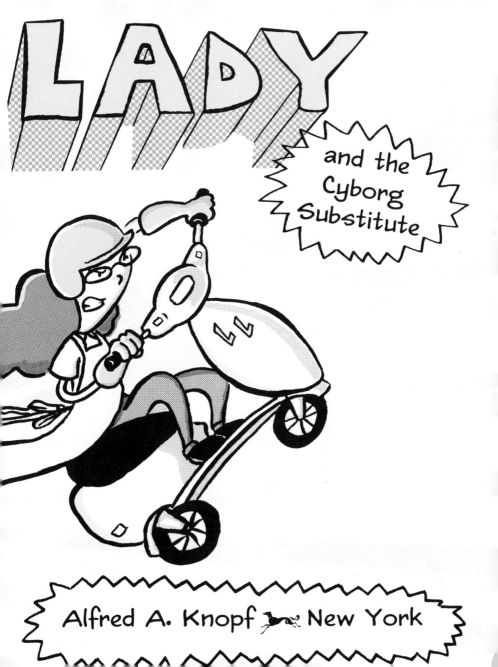

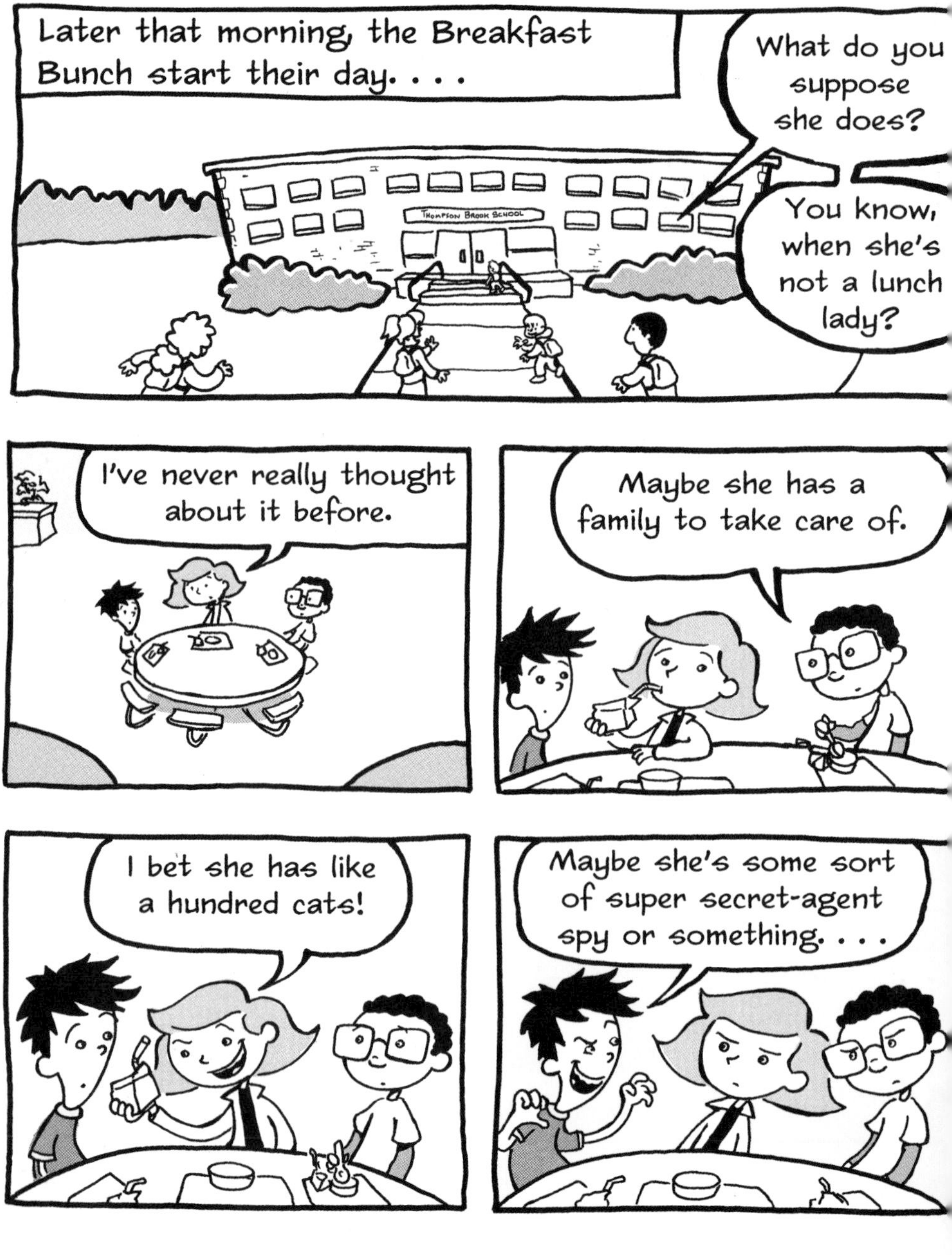
Later that morning, the Breakfast Bunch start their day. . . .
THOMPSON BROOK SCHOOL
What do you suppose she does?
You know, when she's not a lunch lady?
I've never really thought about it before.
Maybe she has a family to take care of.
I bet she has like a hundred cats!
Maybe she's some sort of super secret-agent spy or something. . . .

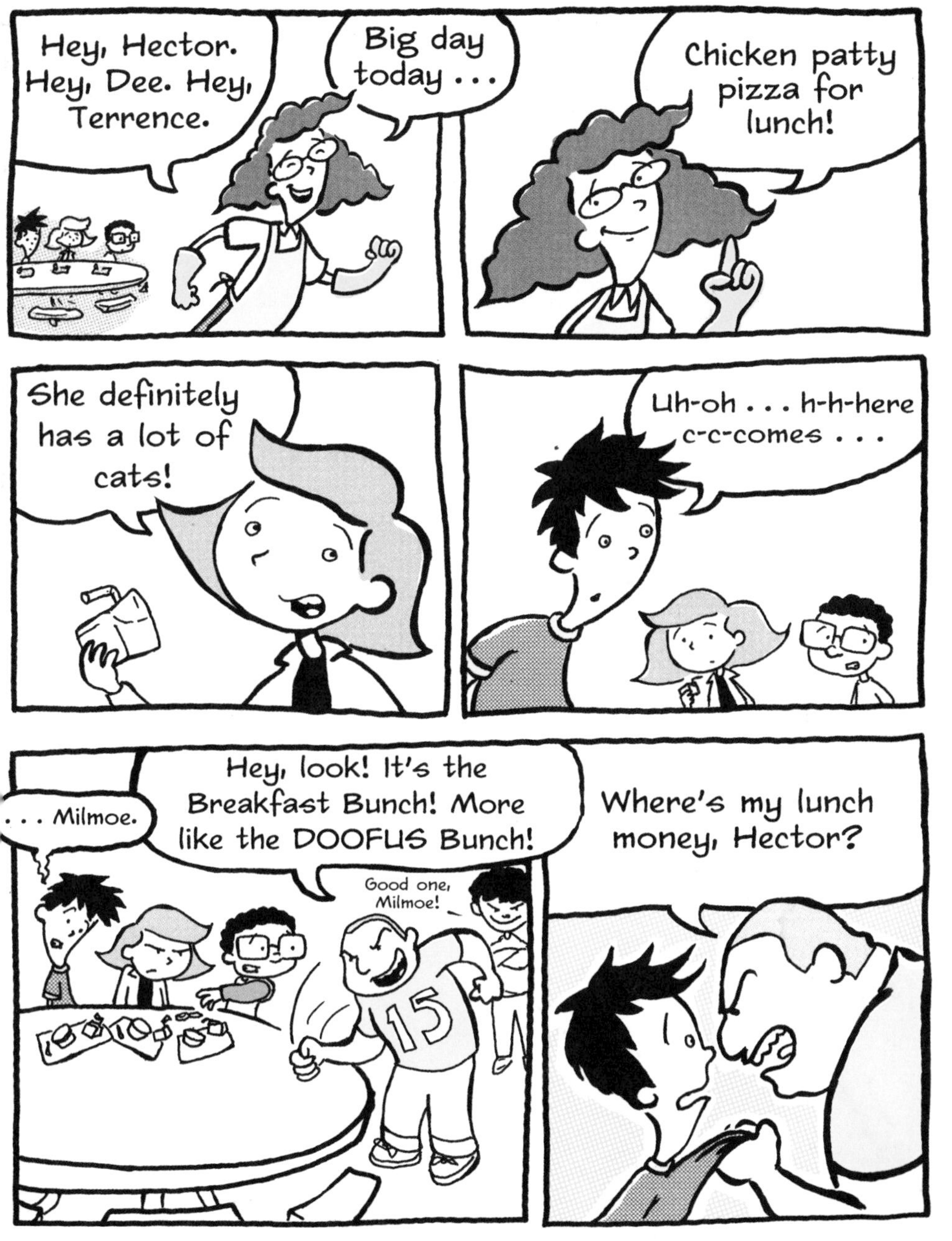
Hey, Hector. Hey, Dee. Hey, Terrence.
Big day today . . .
Chicken patty pizza for lunch!
She definitely has a lot of cats!
Uh-oh . . . h-h-here c-c-comes . . .
. . . Milmoe.
Hey, look! It's the Breakfast Bunch! More like the DOOFUS Bunch!
Good one, Milmoe!
15
Where's my lunch money, Hector?

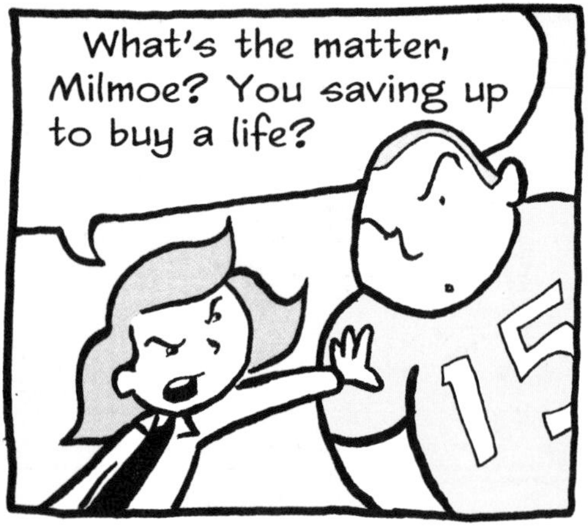
What's the matter, Milmoe? You saving up to buy a life?

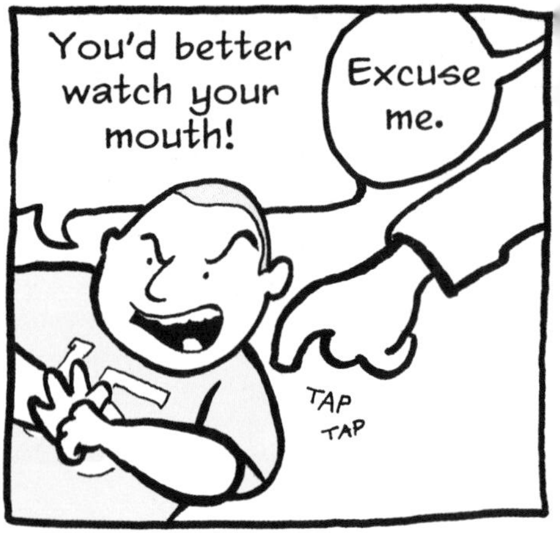
You'd better watch your mouth!
Excuse me.
TAP TAP

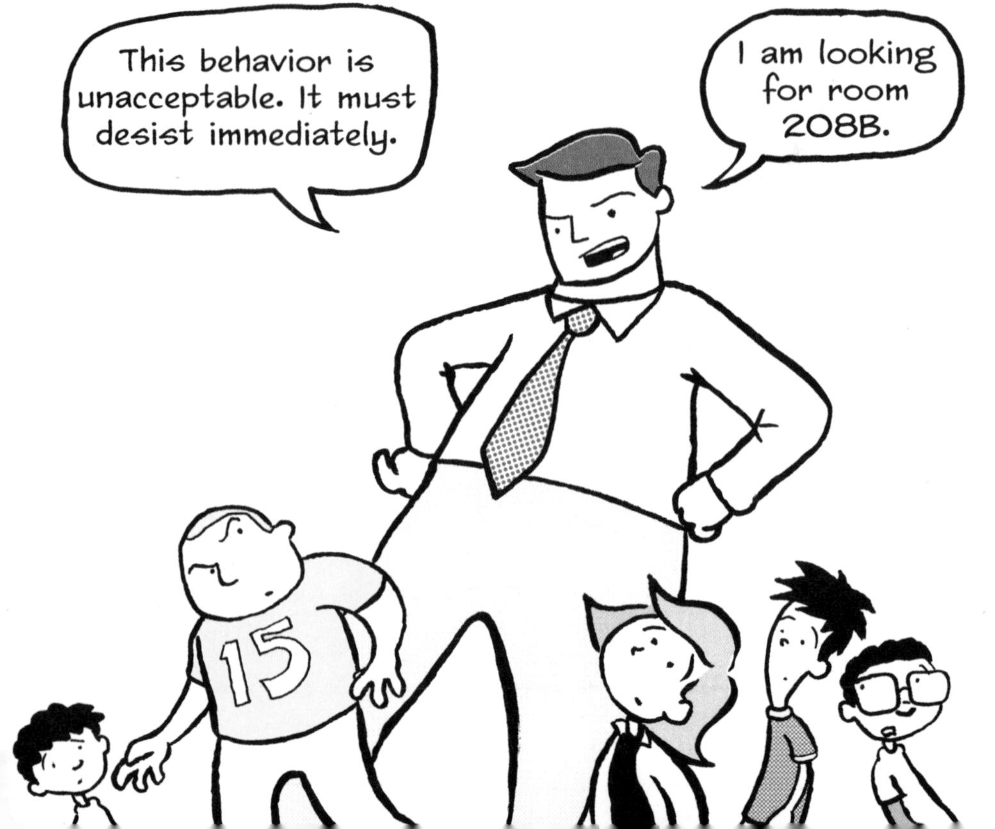
I am looking for room 208B.
This behavior is unacceptable. It must desist immediately.

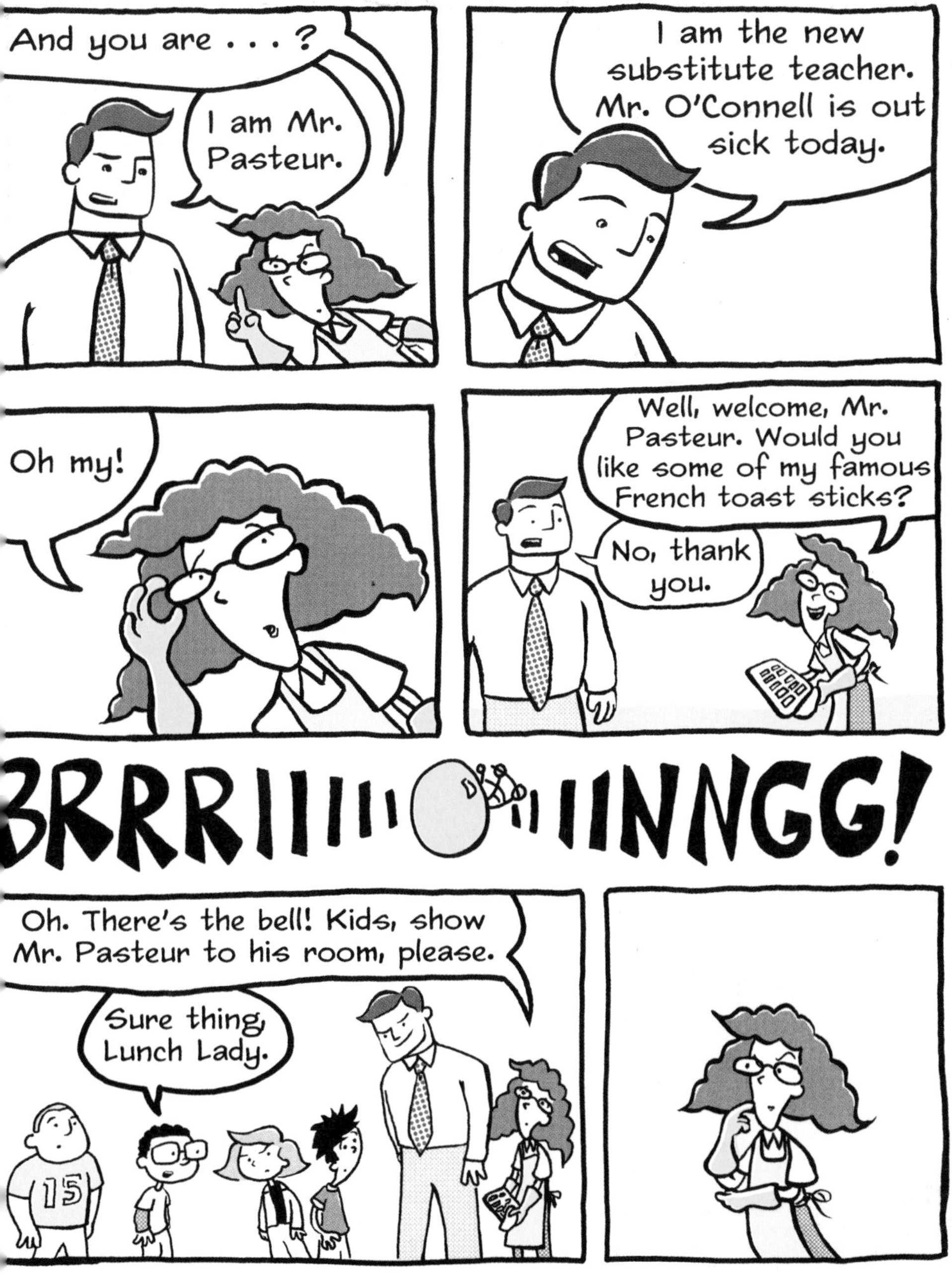
And you are . . . ?
I am Mr. Pasteur.
I am the new substitute teacher. Mr. O'Connell is out sick today.
Oh my!
Well, welcome, Mr. Pasteur. Would you like some of my famous French toast sticks?
No, thank you.
BRRRIIIIIIINNGG!
Oh. There's the bell! Kids, show Mr. Pasteur to his room, please.
Sure thing, Lunch Lady.
15

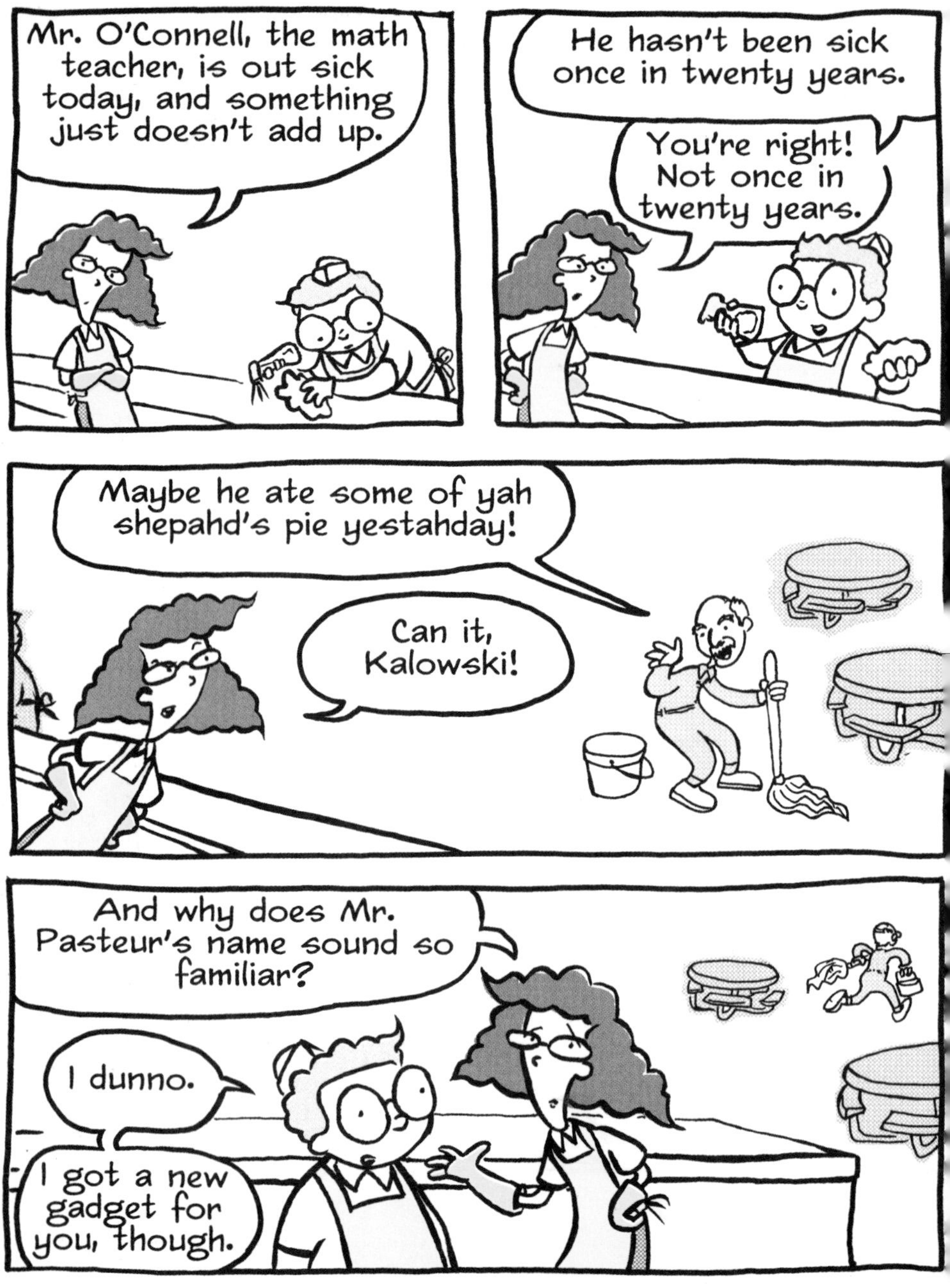
Mr. O'Connell, the math teacher, is out sick today, and something just doesn't add up.
He hasn't been sick once in twenty years.
You're right! Not once in twenty years.
Maybe he ate some of yah shepahd's pie yestahday!
Can it, Kalowski!
And why does Mr. Pasteur's name sound so familiar?
I dunno.
I got a new gadget for you, though.

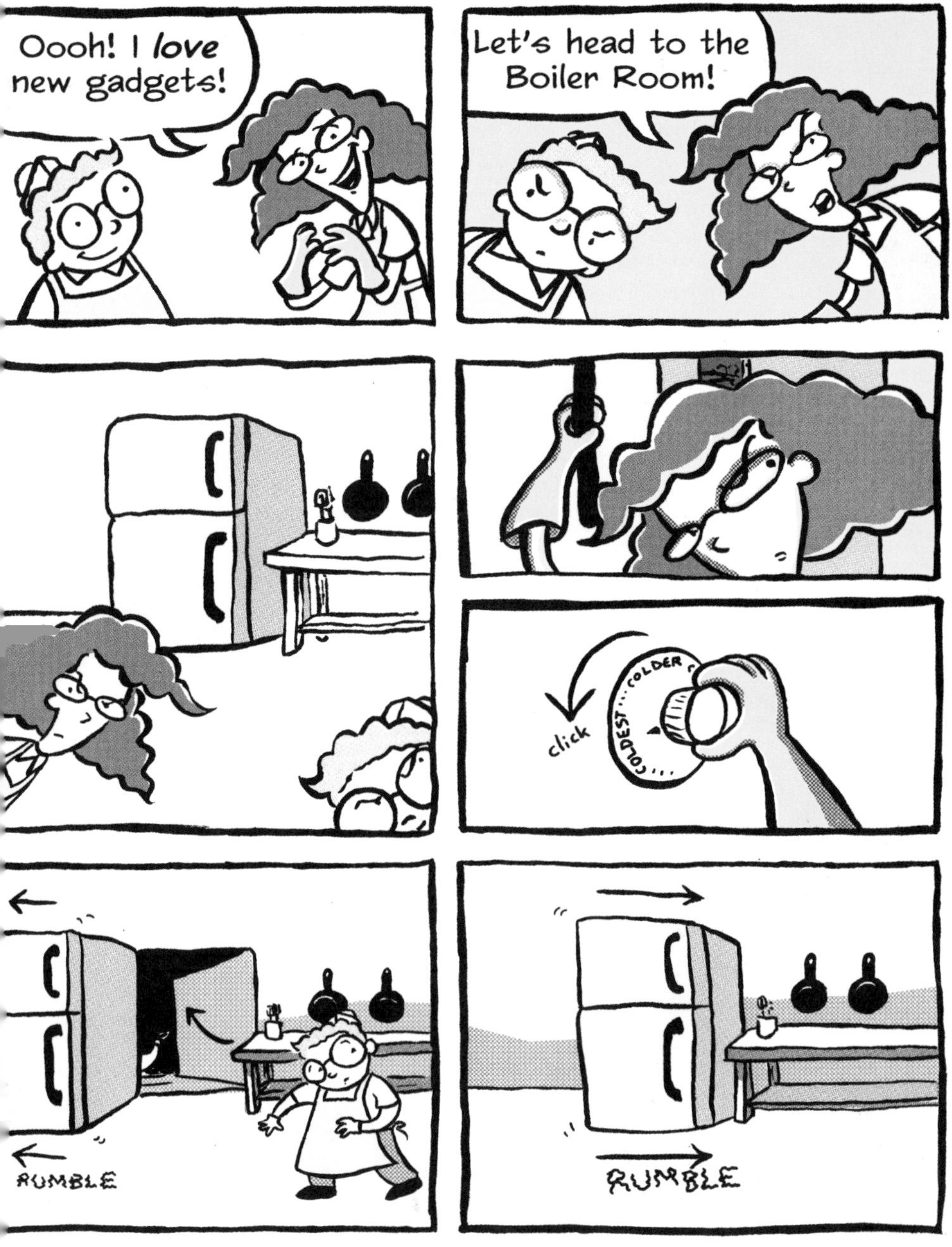

Oooh! I *love* new gadgets!
Let's head to the Boiler Room!
COLDER
COLDEST
click
RUMBLE
RUMBLE

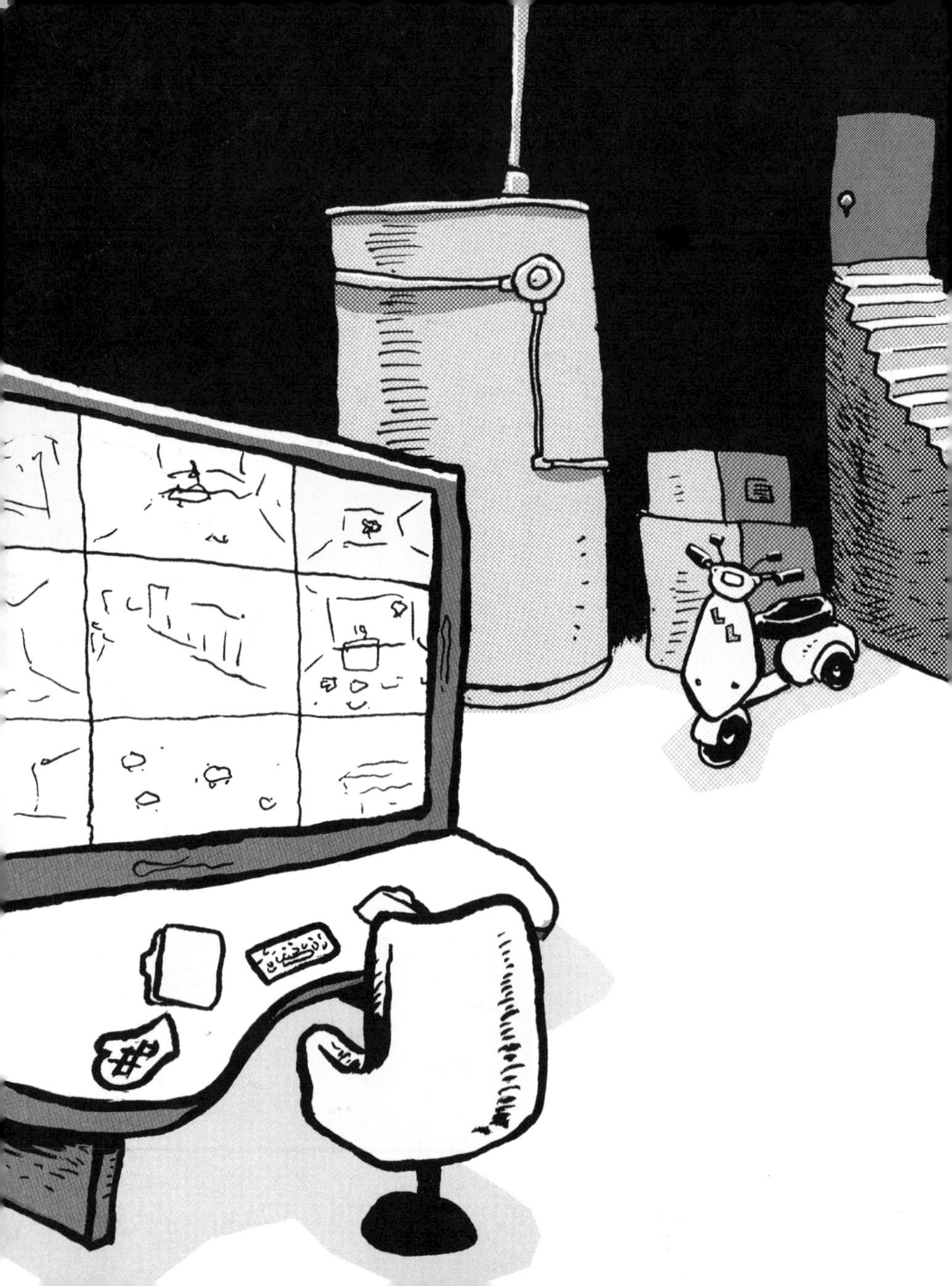

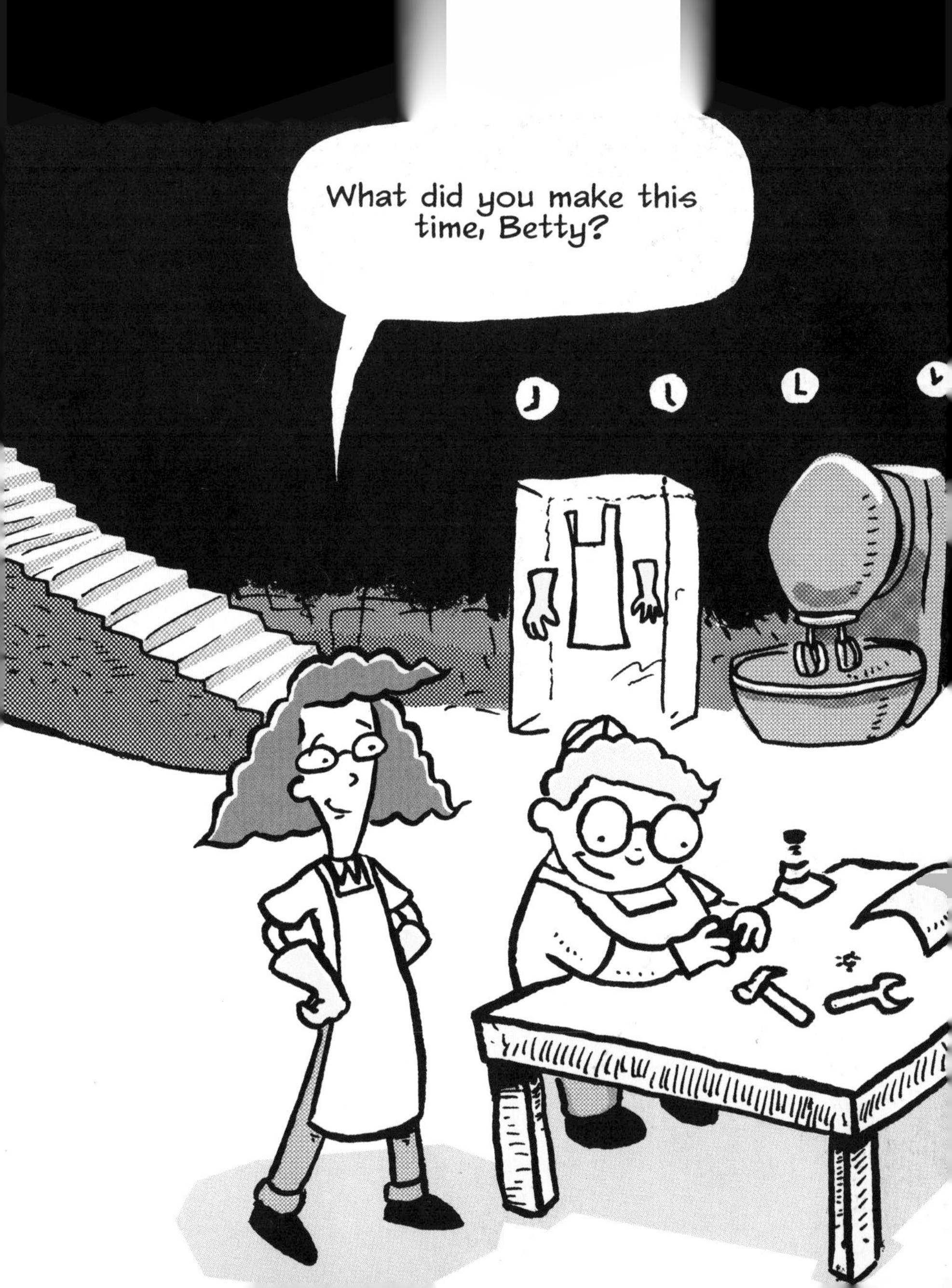
What did you make this time, Betty?

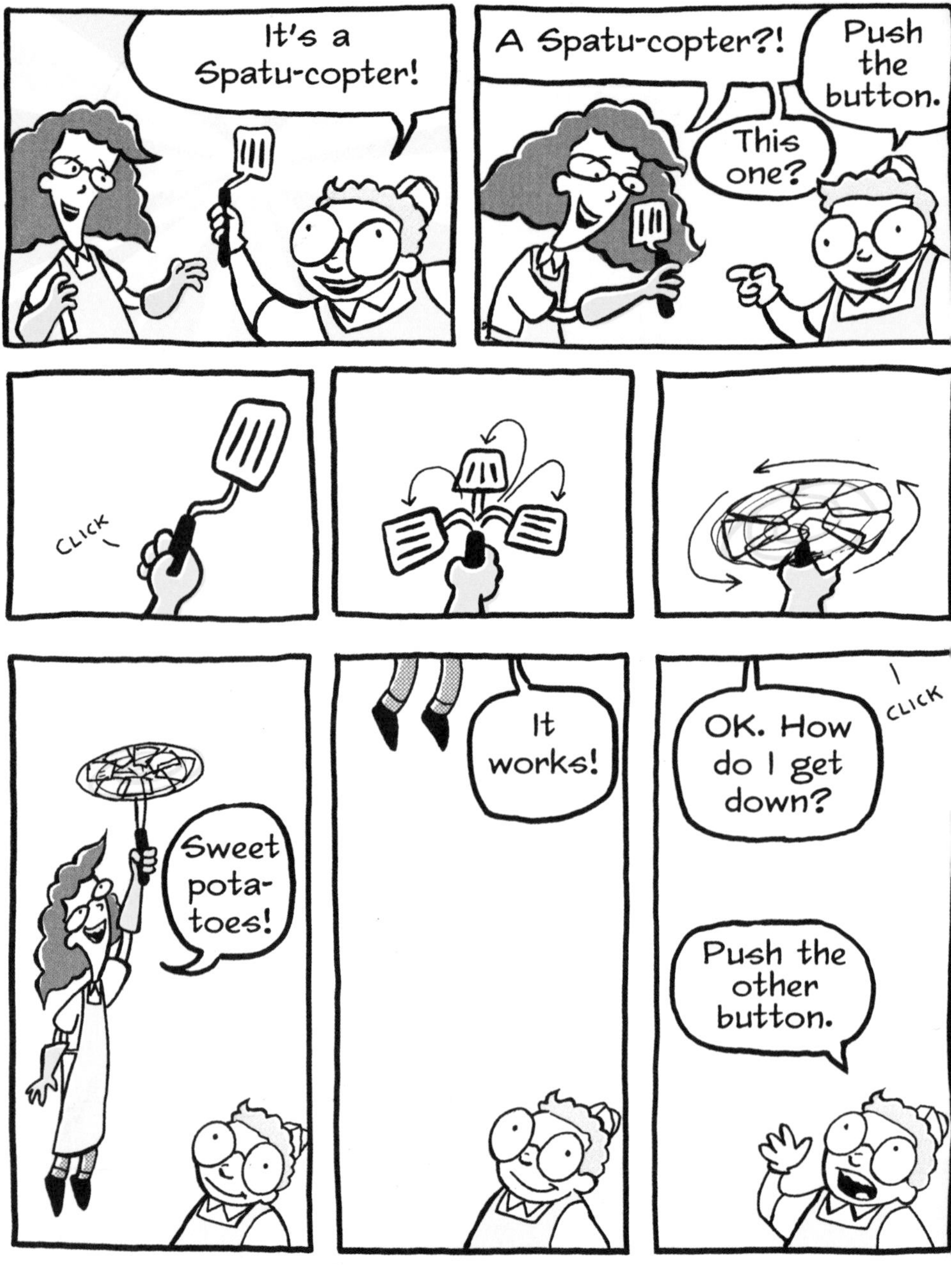
It's a Spatu-copter!
A Spatu-copter?!
This one?
Push the button.
CLICK
Sweet pota-toes!
It works!
OK. How do I get down?
CLICK
Push the other button.

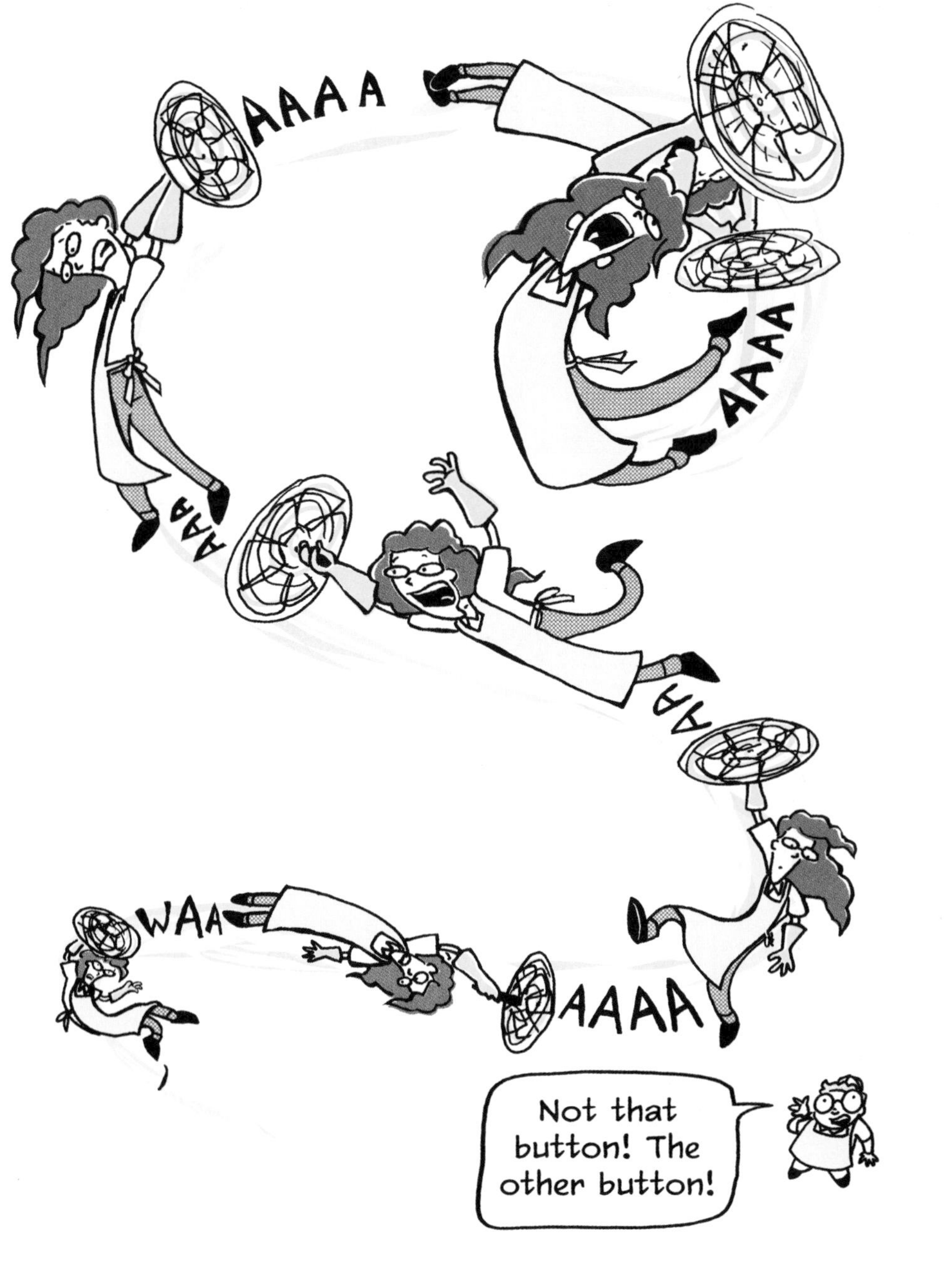
AAAA
AAAA
AAA
AA
WAA
AAAA
Not that button! The other button!

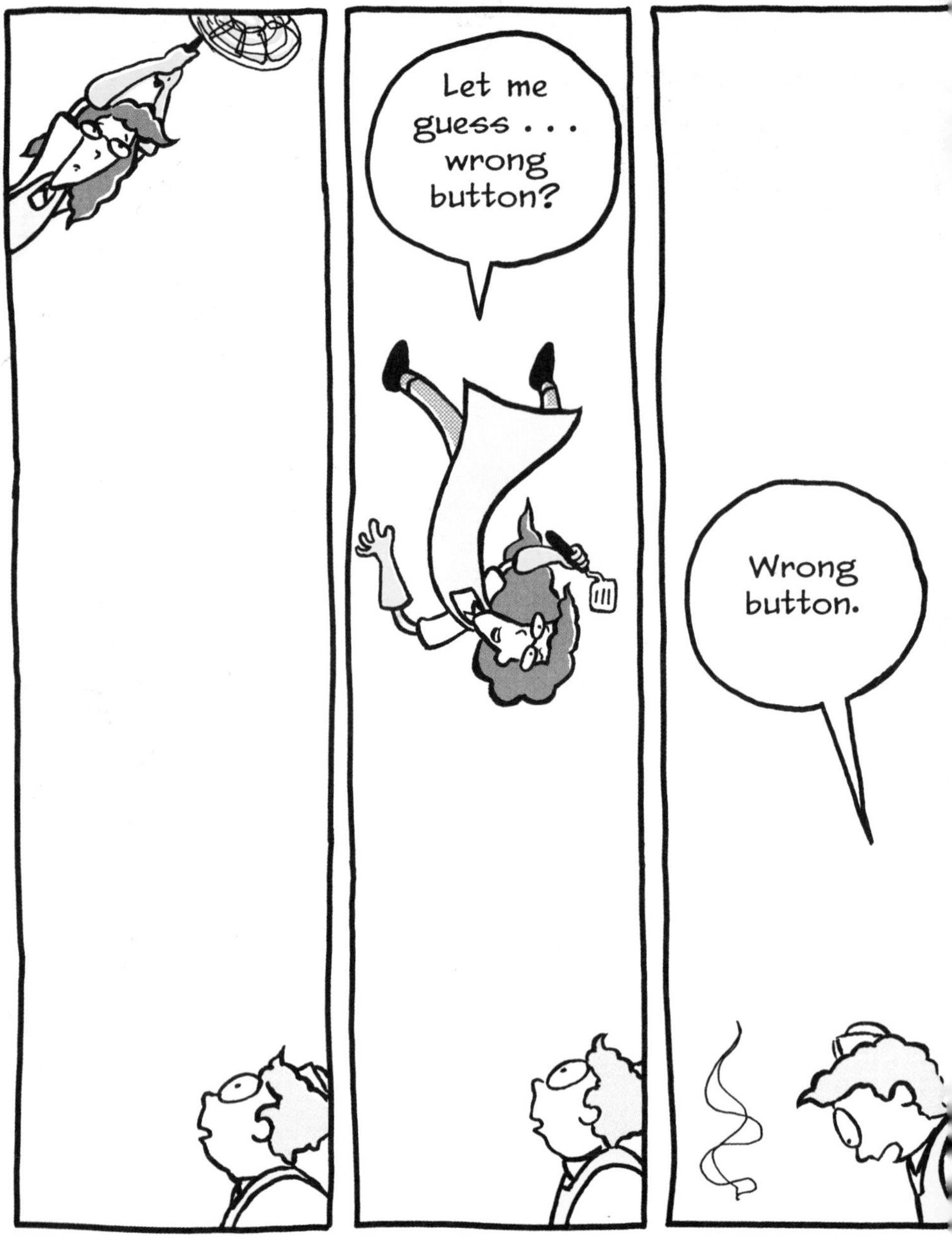
Let me guess . . . wrong button?
Wrong button.

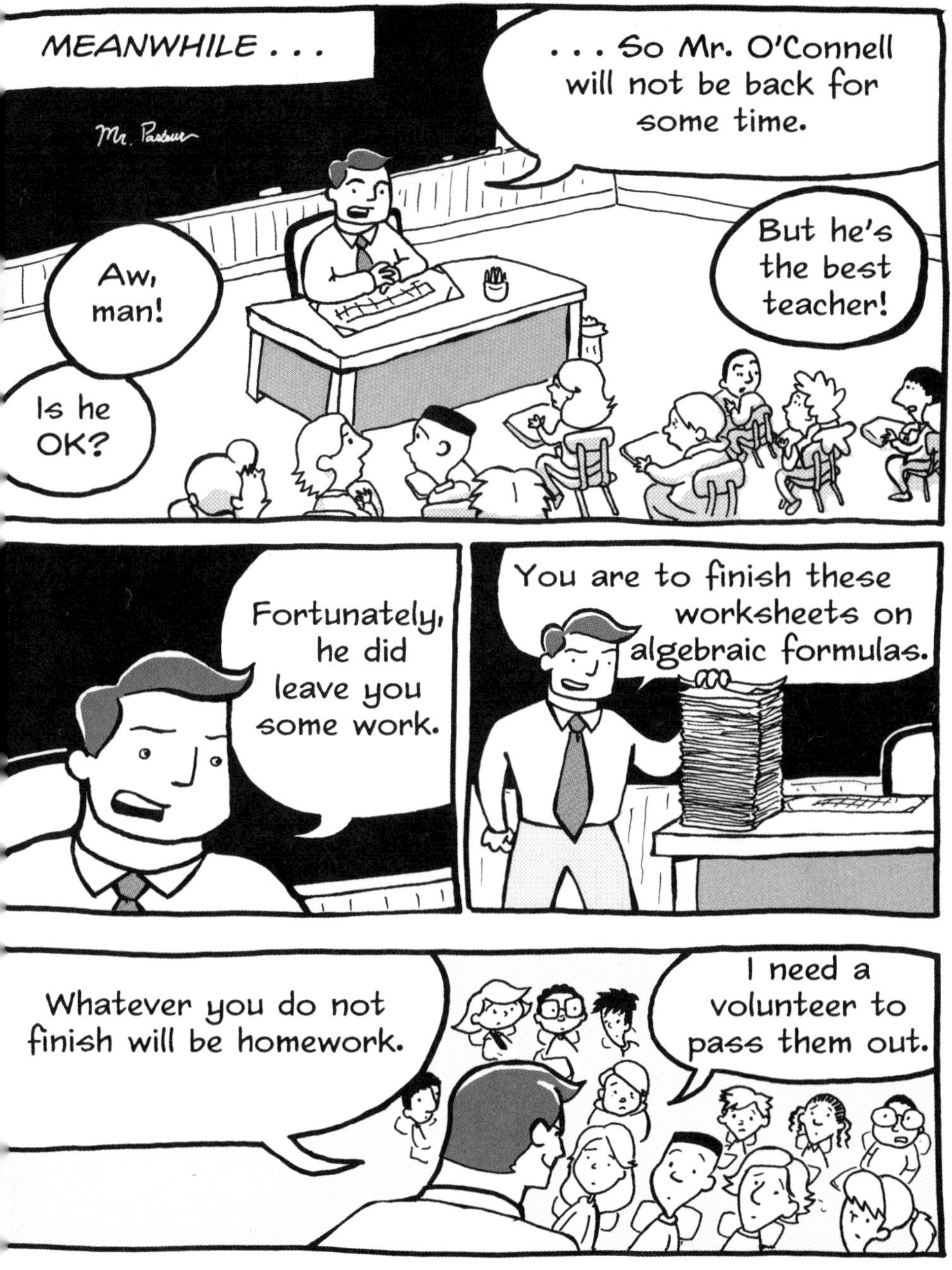
MEANWHILE . . .
Mr. Parker
. . . So Mr. O'Connell will not be back for some time.
Aw, man!
Is he OK?
But he's the best teacher!
Fortunately, he did leave you some work.
You are to finish these worksheets on algebraic formulas.
Whatever you do not finish will be homework.
I need a volunteer to pass them out.

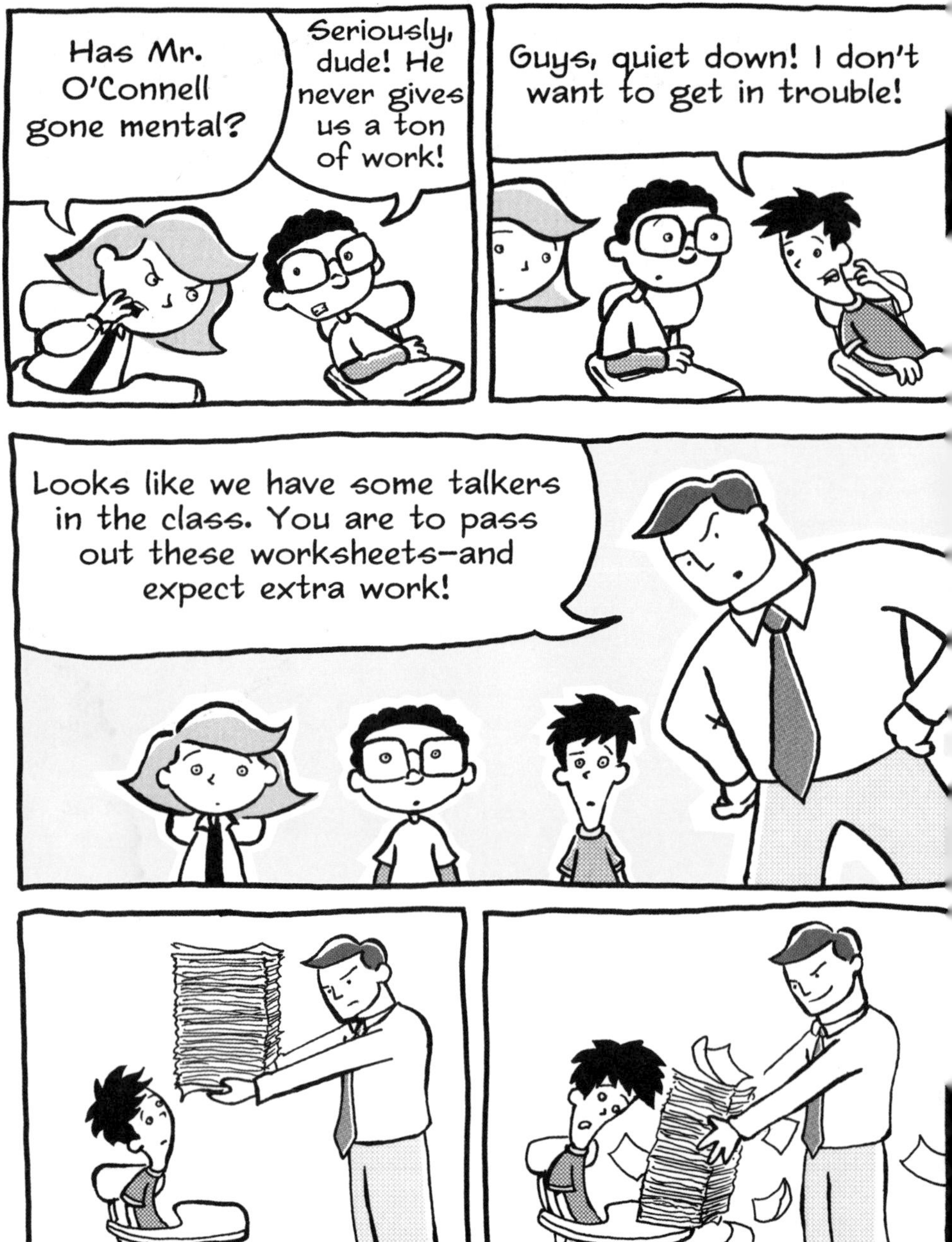
Has Mr. O'Connell gone mental?
Seriously, dude! He never gives us a ton of work!
Guys, quiet down! I don't want to get in trouble!
Looks like we have some talkers in the class. You are to pass out these worksheets—and expect extra work!

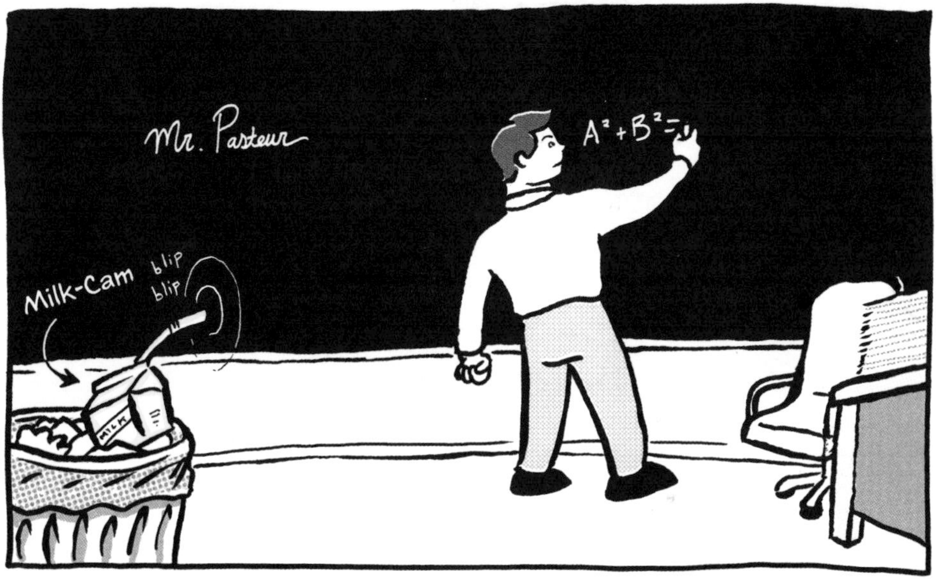
Mr. Pasteur
A²+B²=
Milk-Cam
blip
blip
MILK

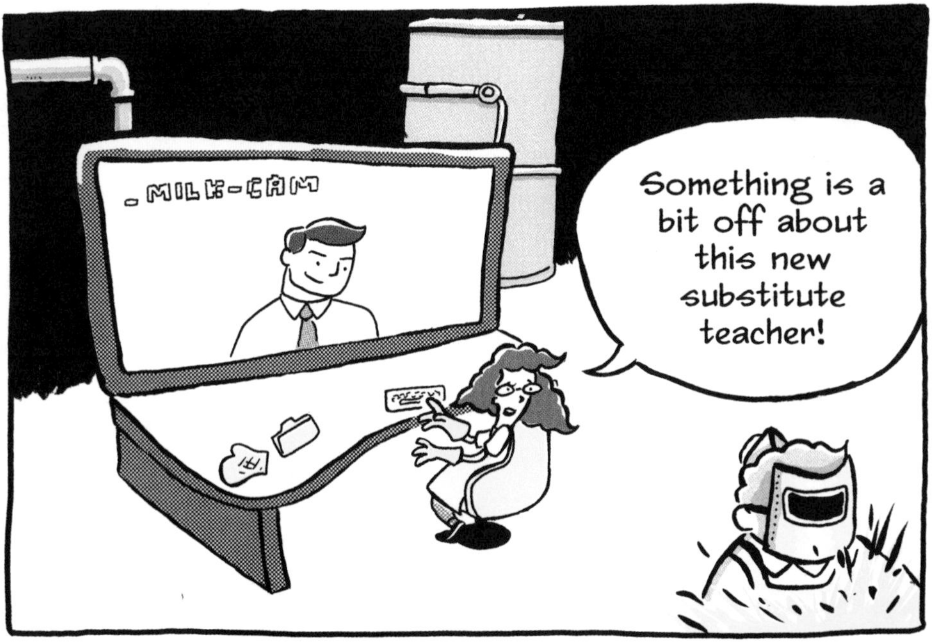
MILK-CAM
Something is a bit off about this new substitute teacher!

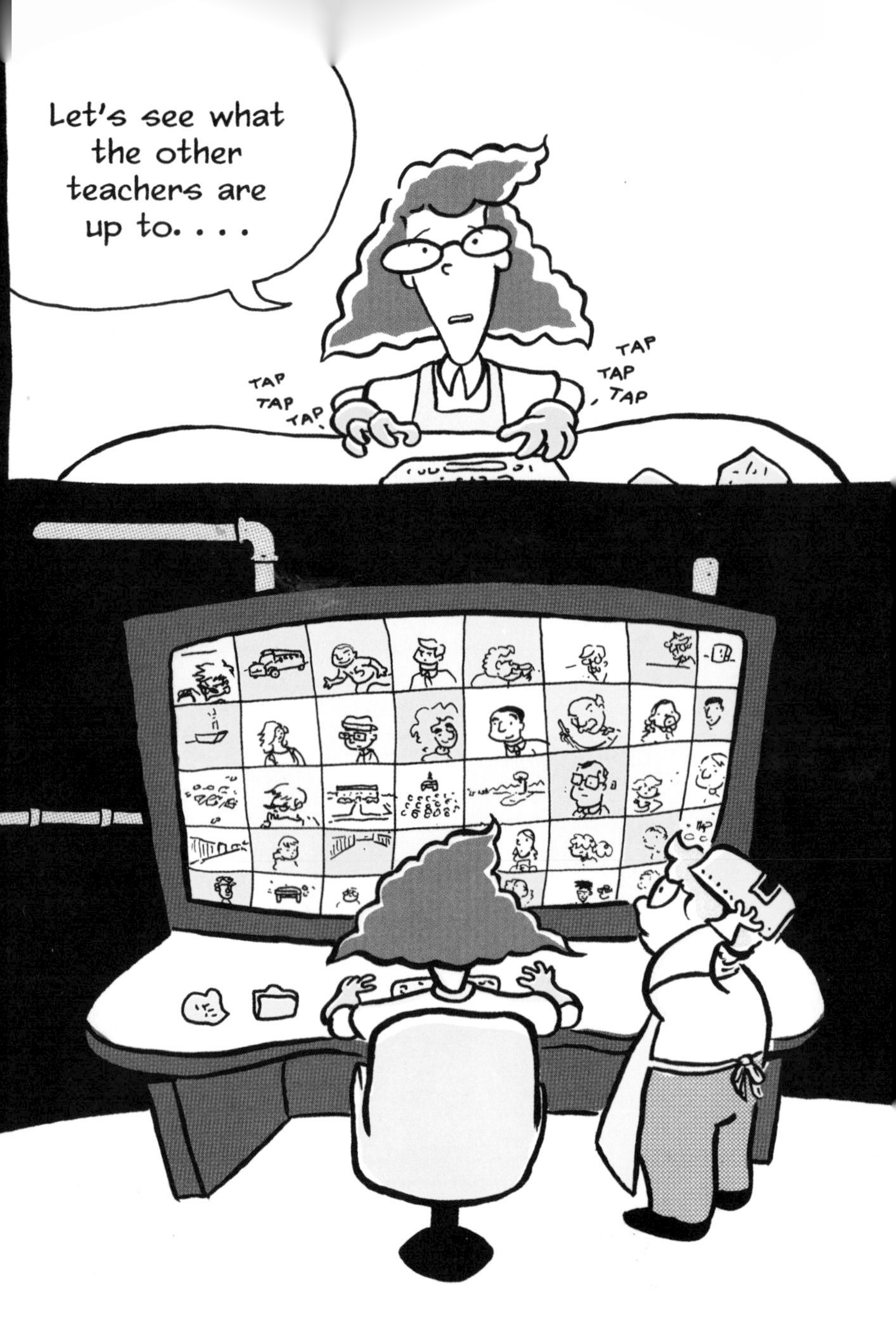
Let's see what the other teachers are up to. . . .
TAP
TAP
TAP
TAP
TAP
TAP

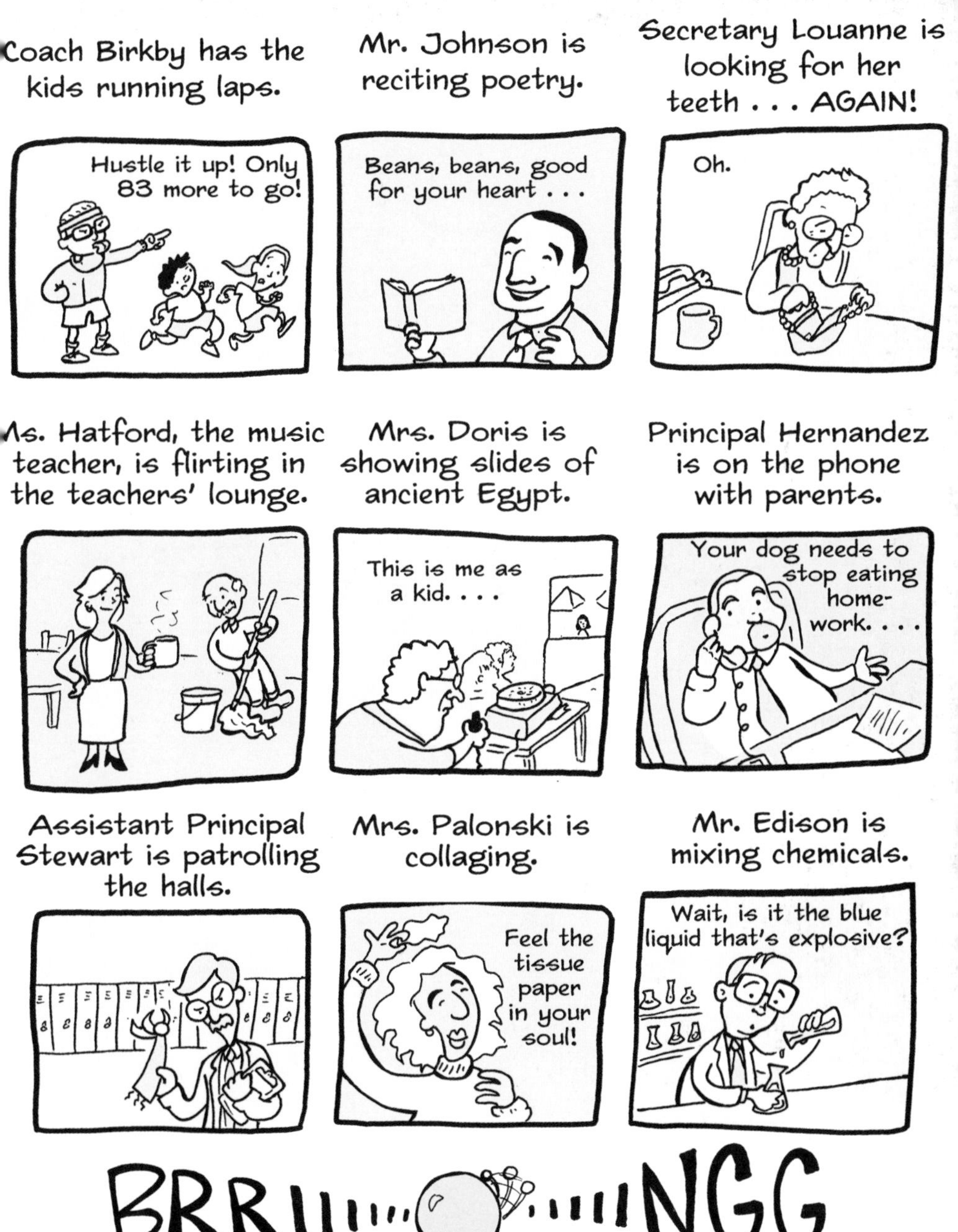
Coach Birkby has the kids running laps.
Hustle it up! Only 83 more to go!
Mr. Johnson is reciting poetry.
Beans, beans, good for your heart . . .
Secretary Louanne is looking for her teeth . . . AGAIN!
Oh.
Ms. Hatford, the music teacher, is flirting in the teachers' lounge.
Mrs. Doris is showing slides of ancient Egypt.
This is me as a kid. . . .
Principal Hernandez is on the phone with parents.
Your dog needs to stop eating home-work. . . .
Assistant Principal Stewart is patrolling the halls.
Mrs. Palonski is collaging.
Feel the tissue paper in your soul!
Mr. Edison is mixing chemicals.
Wait, is it the blue liquid that's explosive?
BRRIIIIIIIIIIIINGG

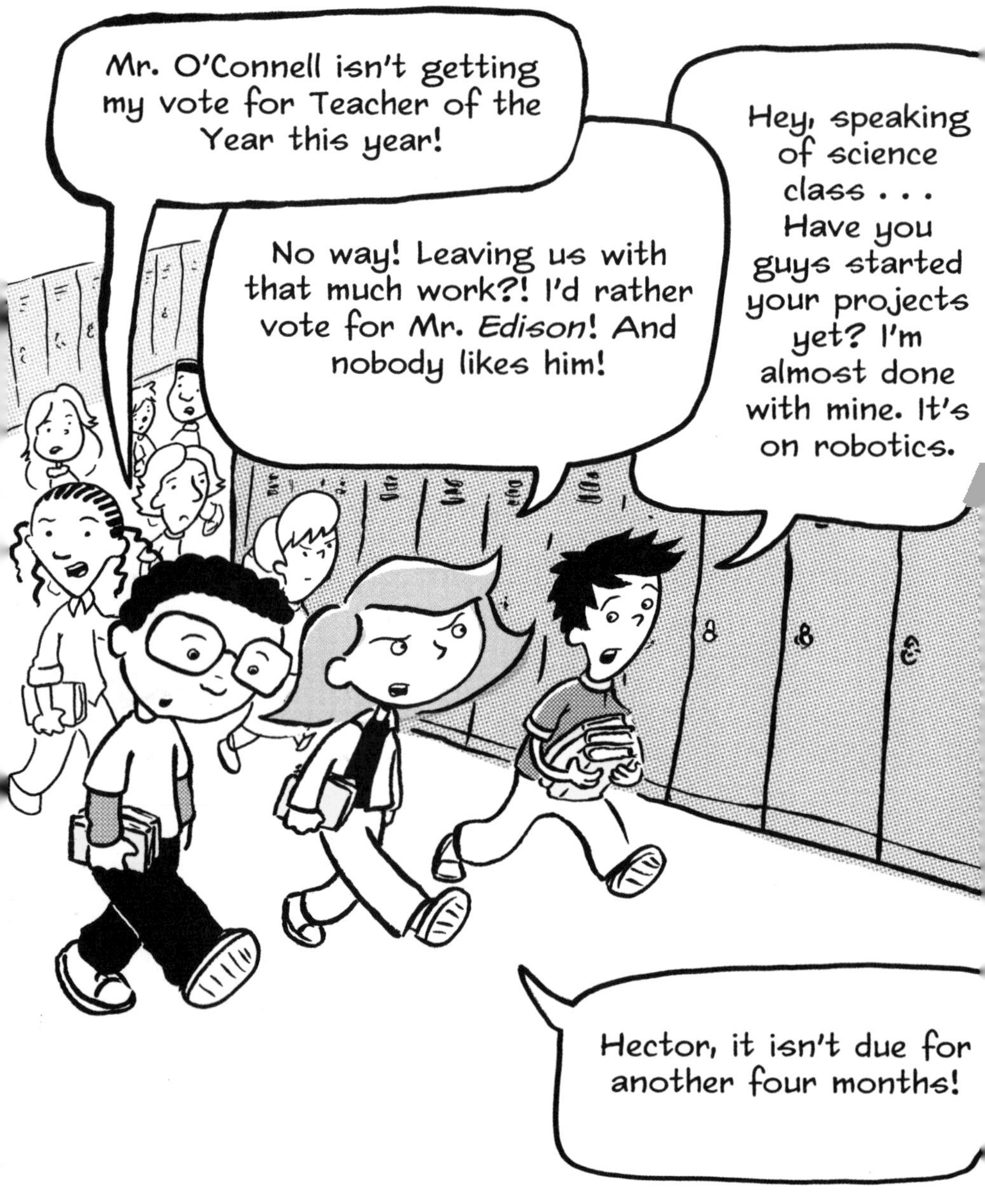

Mr. O'Connell isn't getting my vote for Teacher of the Year this year!
No way! Leaving us with that much work?! I'd rather vote for Mr. *Edison*! And nobody likes him!
Hey, speaking of science class . . . Have you guys started your projects yet? I'm almost done with mine. It's on robotics.
Hector, it isn't due for another four months!

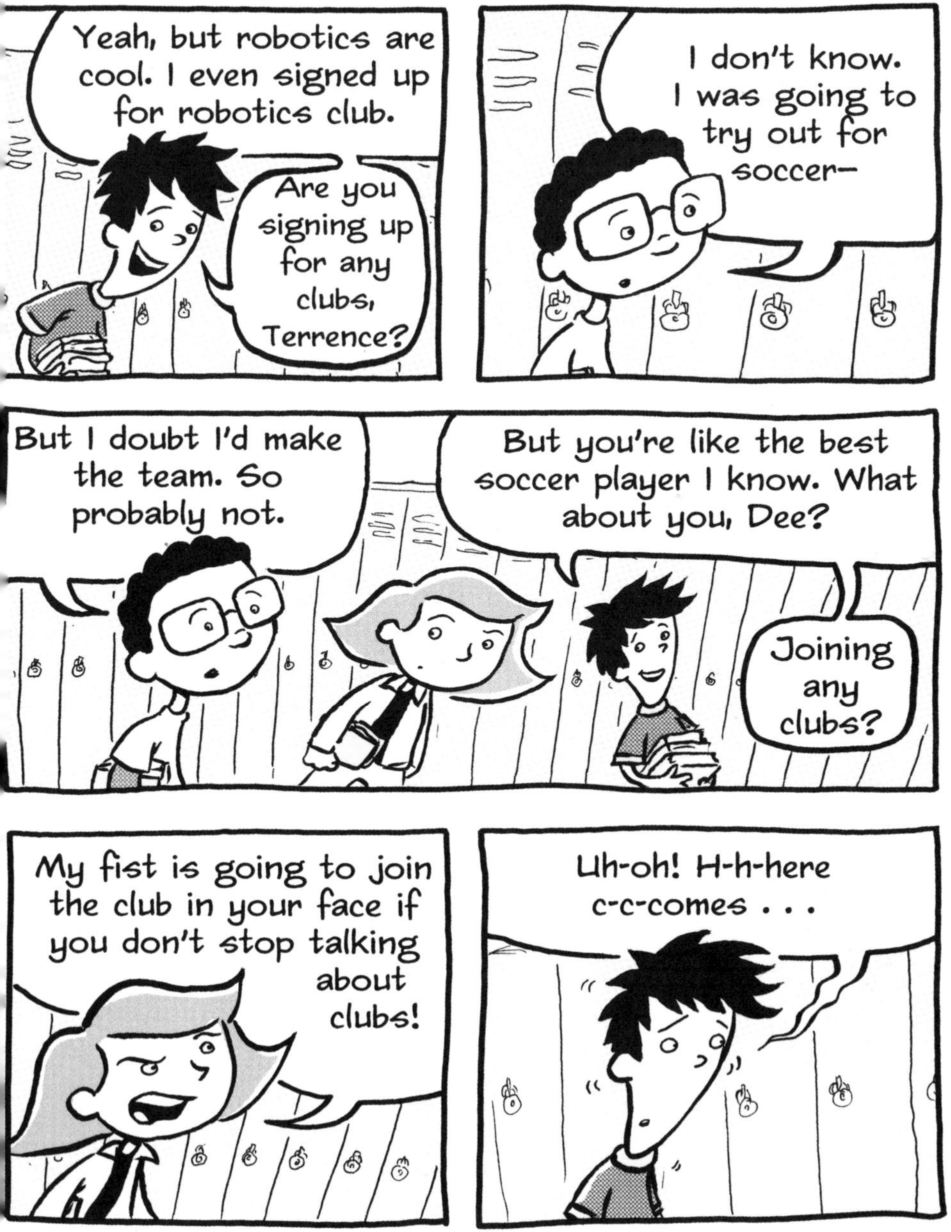
Yeah, but robotics are cool. I even signed up for robotics club.
Are you signing up for any clubs, Terrence?
I don't know. I was going to try out for soccer—
But I doubt I'd make the team. So probably not.
But you're like the best soccer player I know. What about you, Dee?
Joining any clubs?
My fist is going to join the club in your face if you don't stop talking about clubs!
Uh-oh! H-h-here c-c-comes . . .

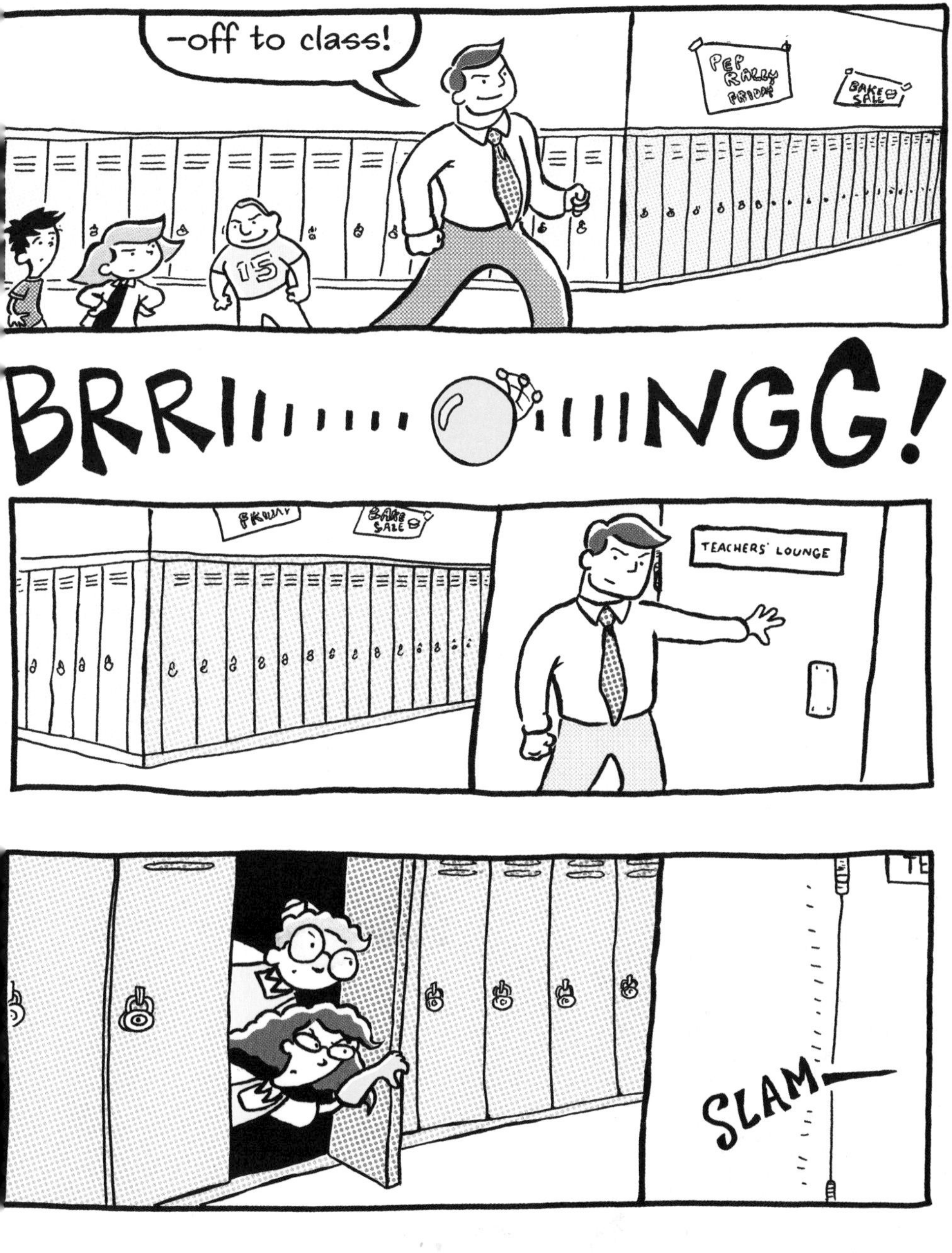

-off to class!
PEP RALLY FRIDAY
BAKE SALE
15
BRRIIIIIIIIIIIINGG!
BAKE SALE
TEACHERS' LOUNGE
SLAM

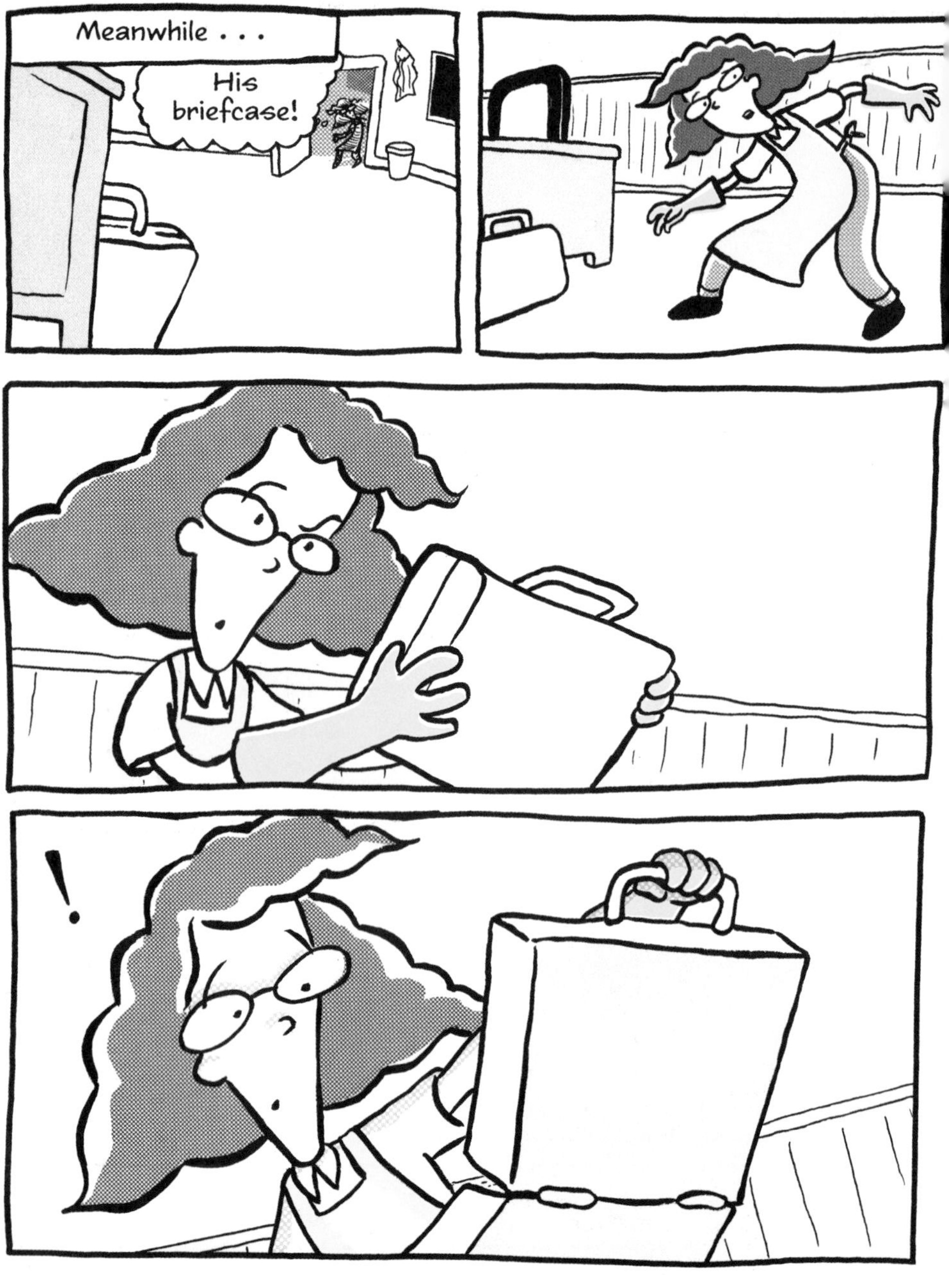
Meanwhile . . .
His briefcase!
!

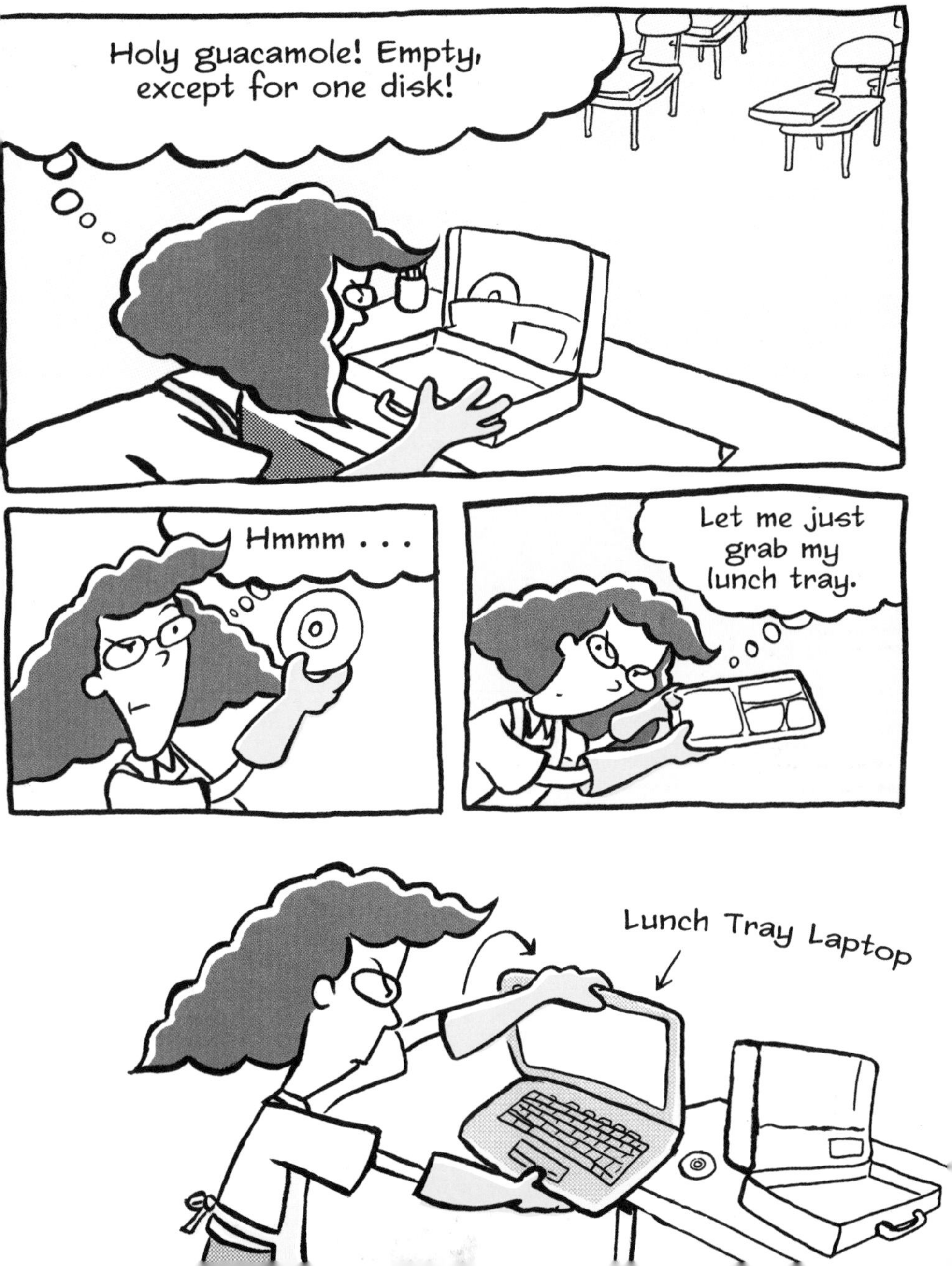
Holy guacamole! Empty, except for one disk!
Hmmm . . .
Let me just grab my lunch tray.
Lunch Tray Laptop

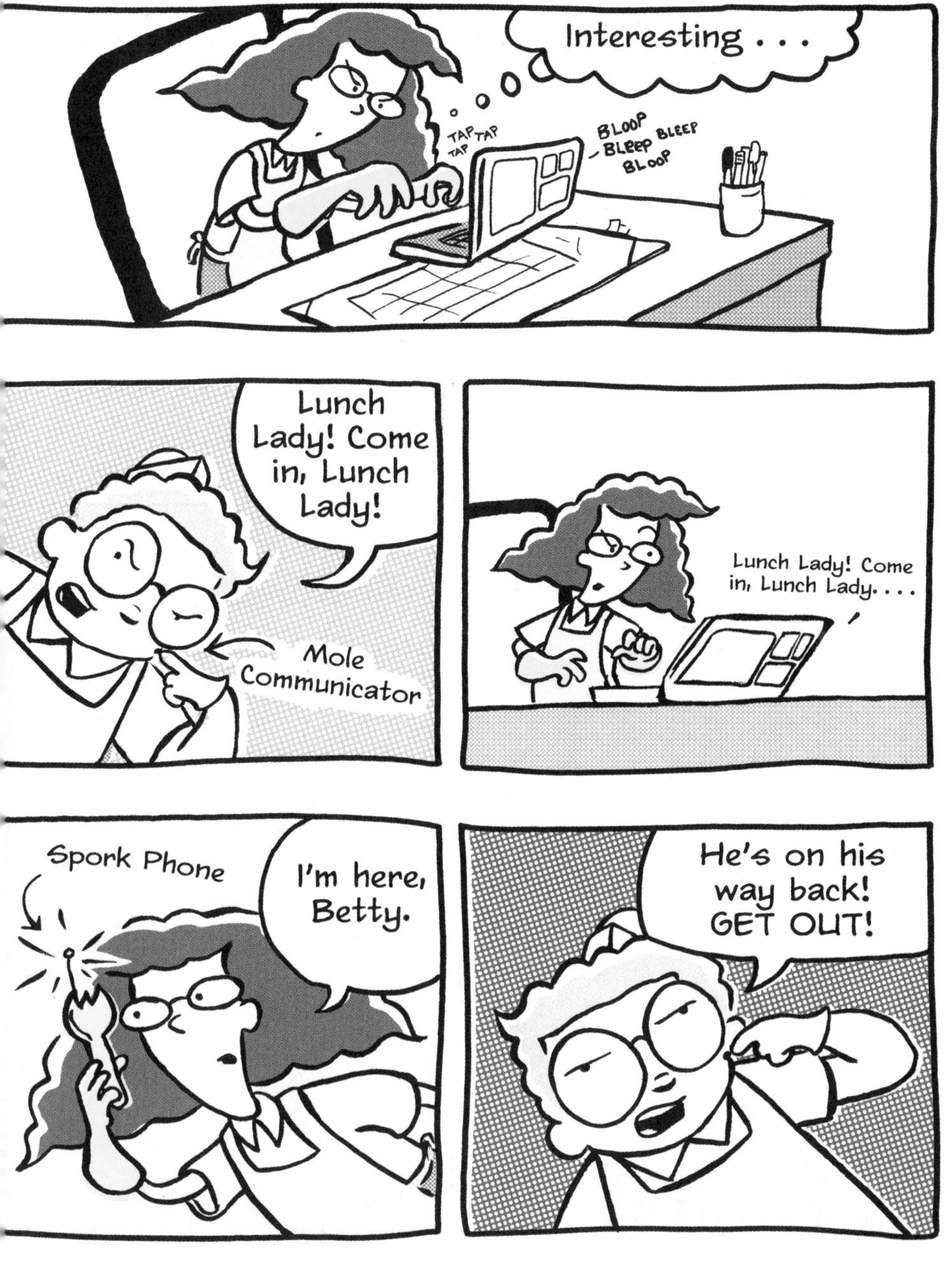
Interesting . . .
TAP TAP TAP
BLOOP BLEEP BLEEP BLOOP
Lunch Lady! Come in, Lunch Lady!
Mole Communicator
Lunch Lady! Come in, Lunch Lady. . . .
Spork Phone
I'm here, Betty.
He's on his way back! GET OUT!

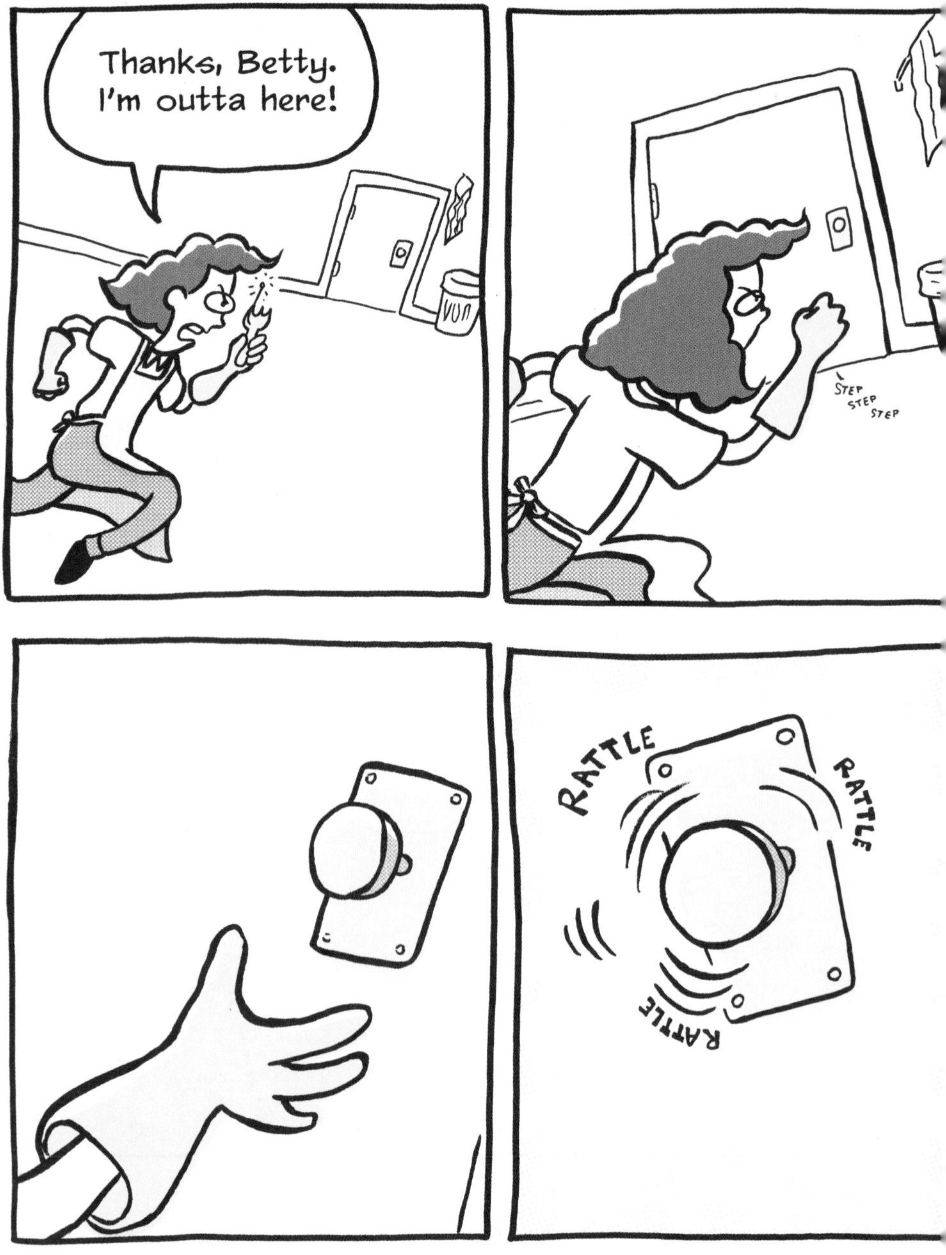

Thanks, Betty. I'm outta here!
STEP STEP STEP
RATTLE
RATTLE
RATTLE

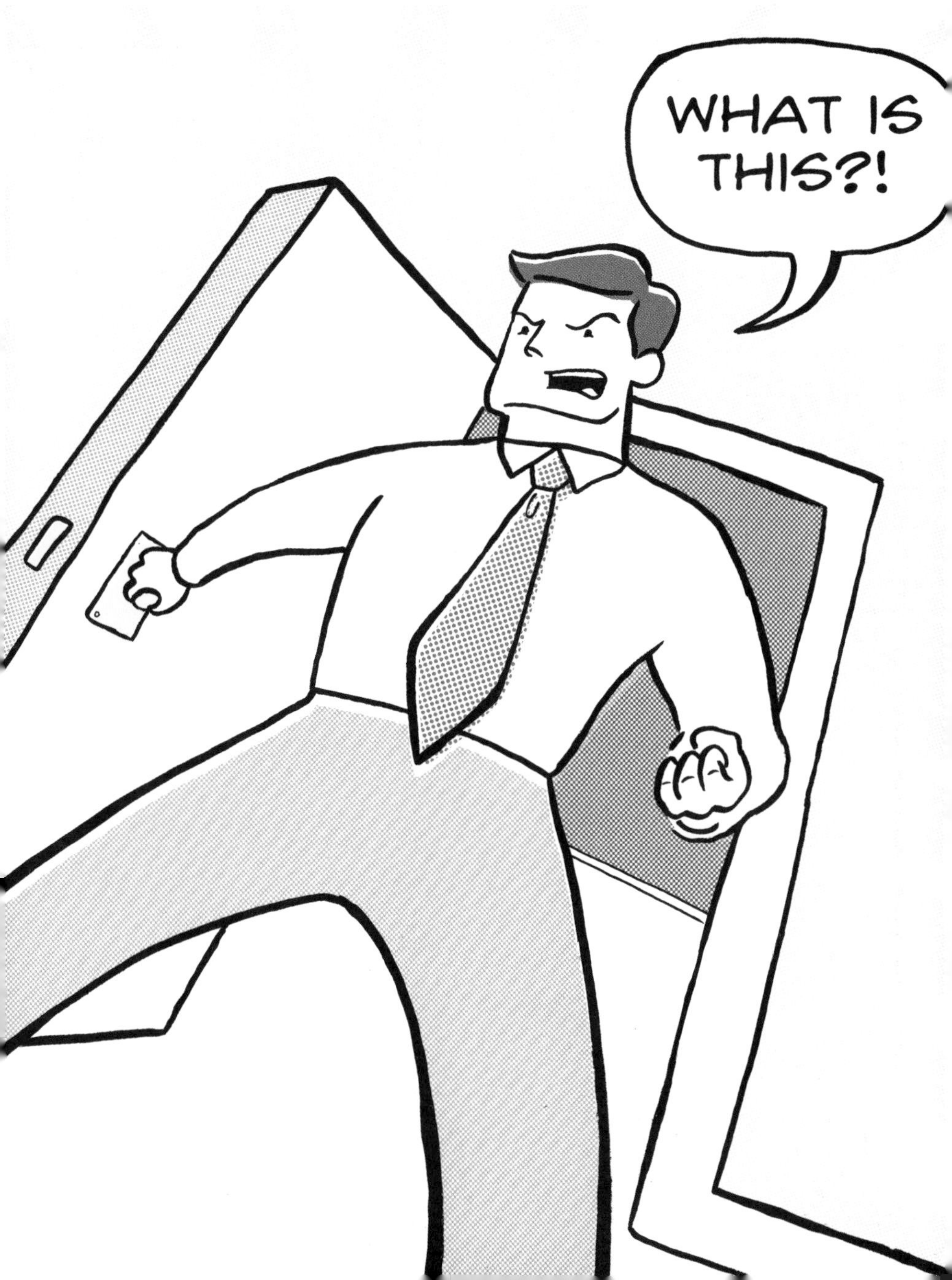
WHAT IS THIS?!

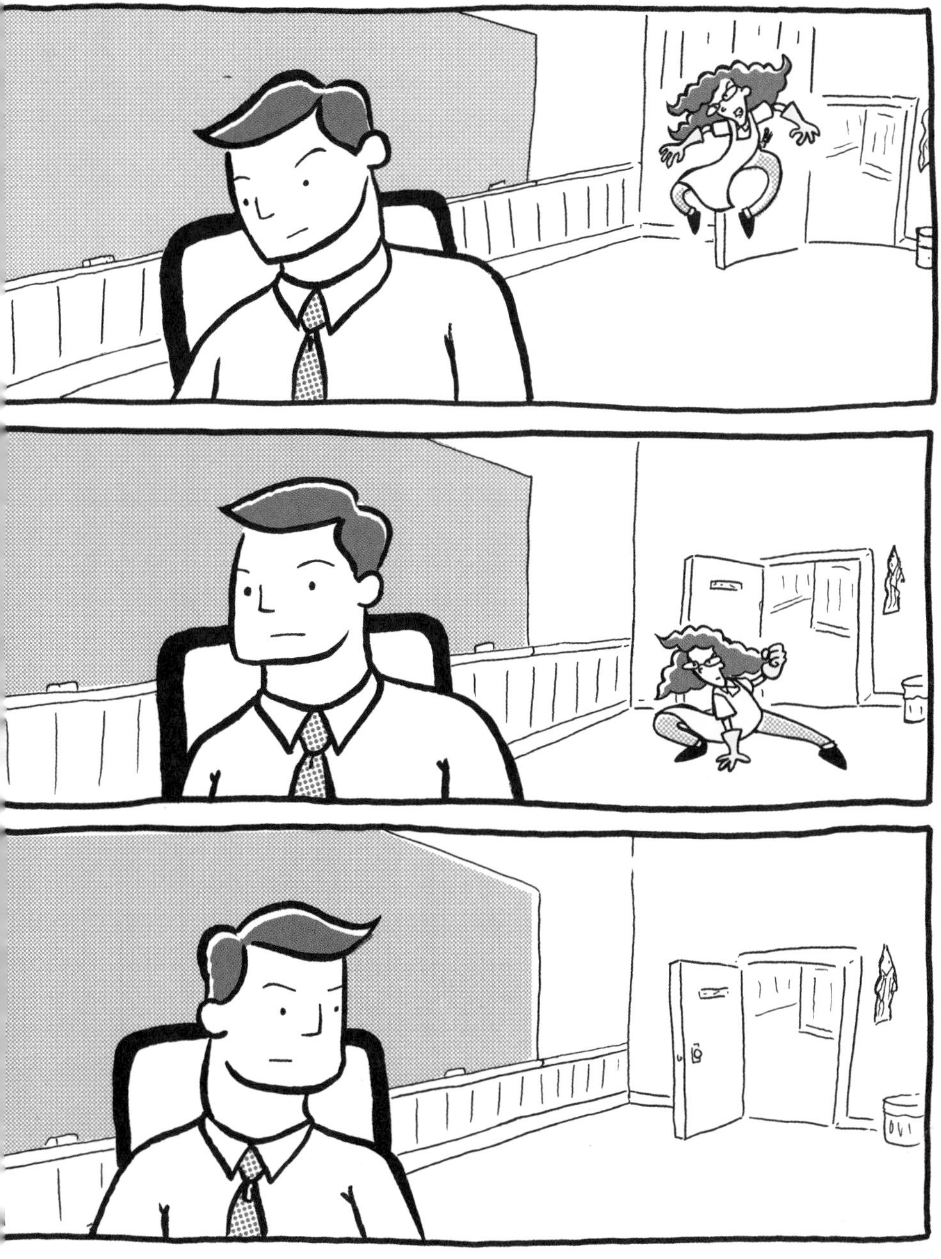

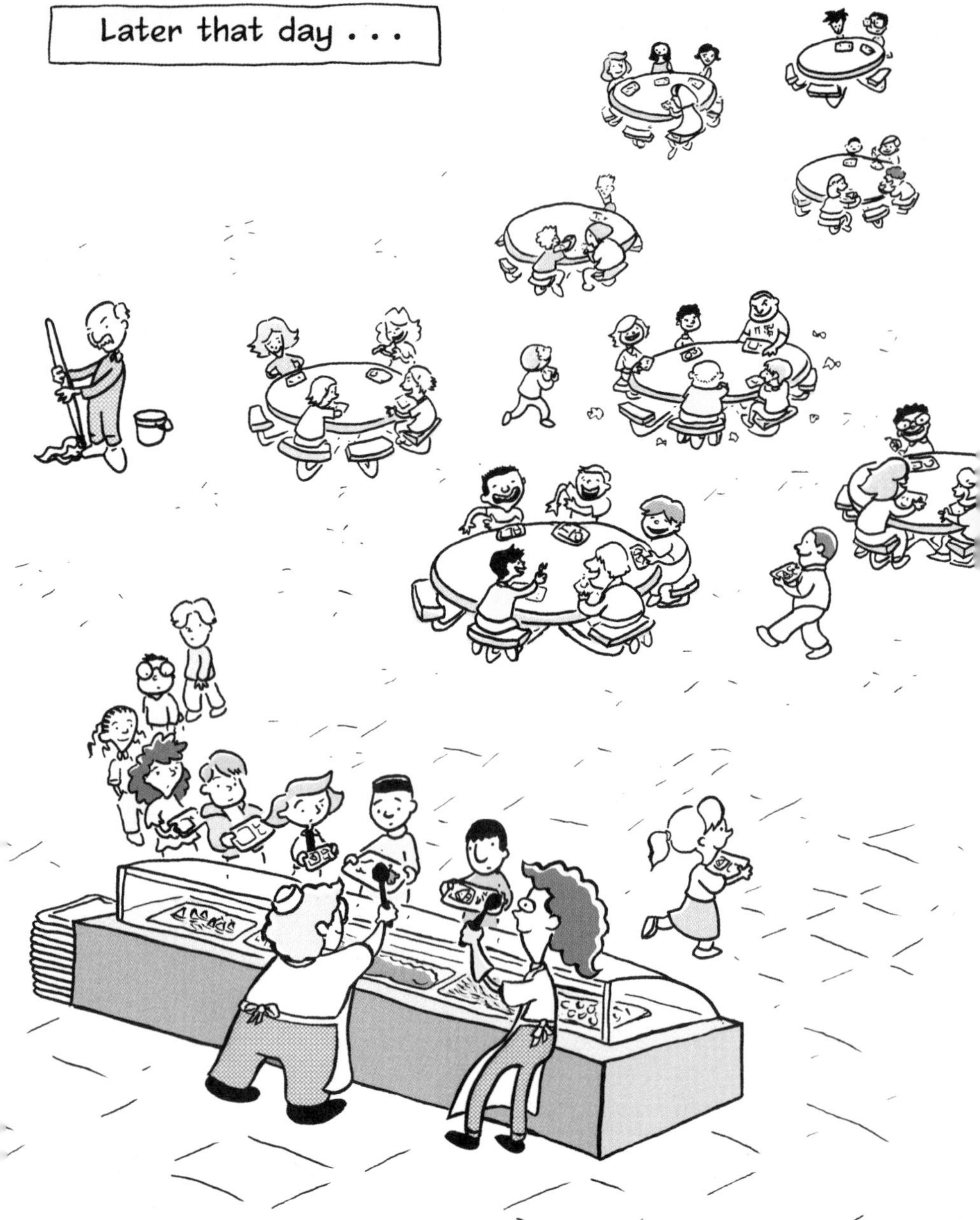
Later that day . . .

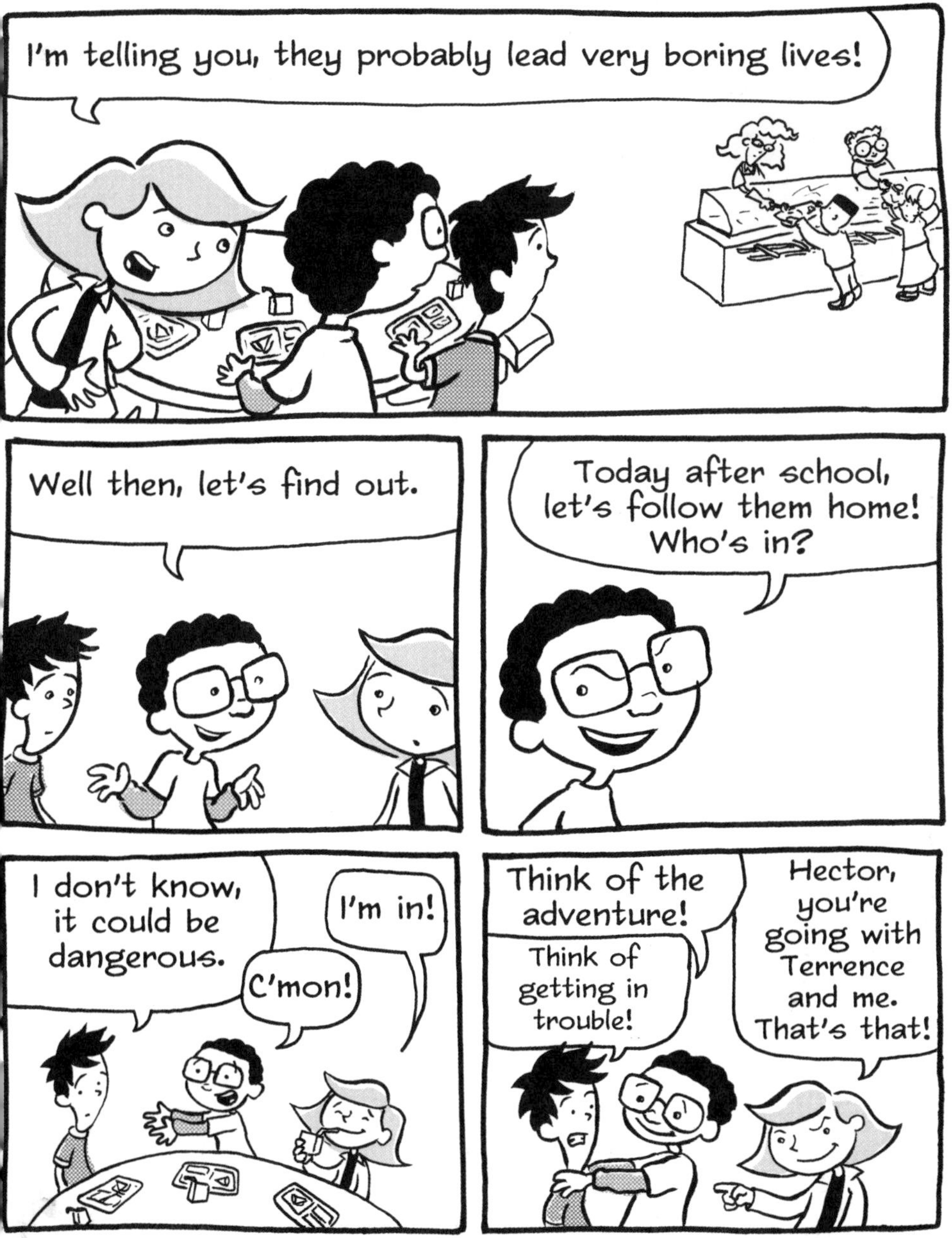
I'm telling you, they probably lead very boring lives!
Well then, let's find out.
Today after school, let's follow them home! Who's in?
I don't know, it could be dangerous.
C'mon!
I'm in!
Think of the adventure!
Think of getting in trouble!
Hector, you're going with Terrence and me. That's that!

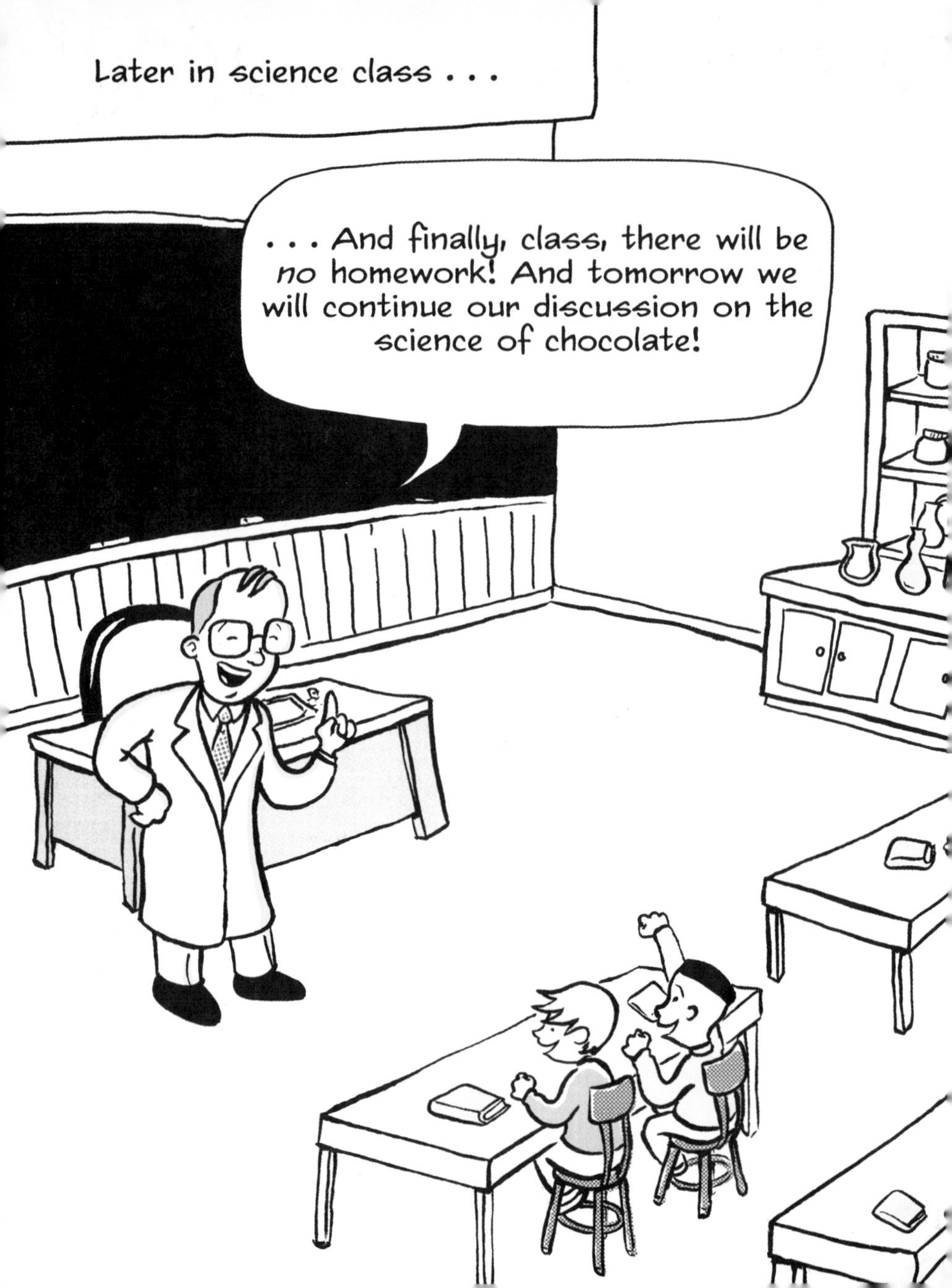
Later in science class . . .
. . . And finally, class, there will be *no* homework! And tomorrow we will continue our discussion on the science of chocolate!

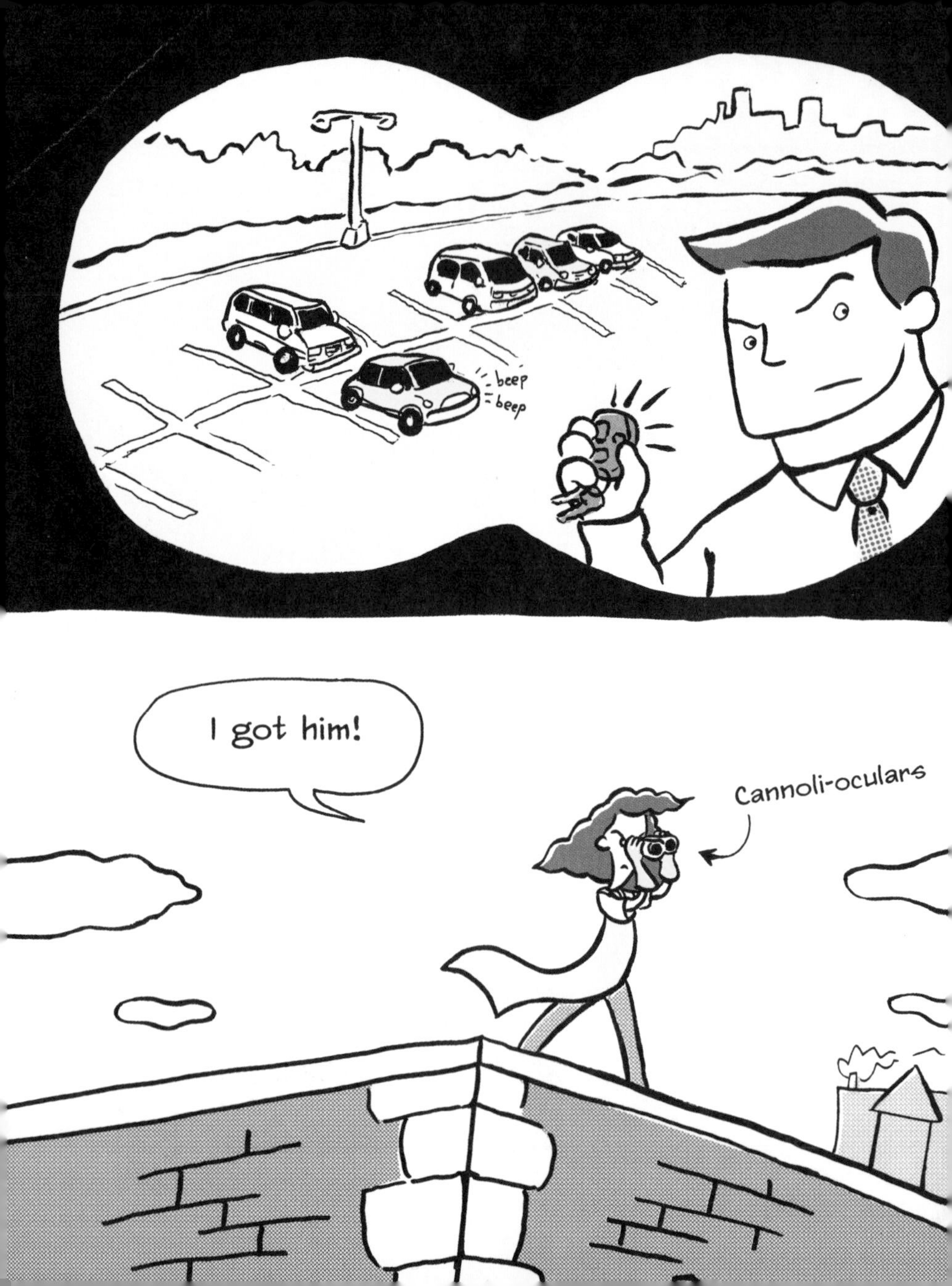
beep
beep
I got him!
Cannoli-oculars

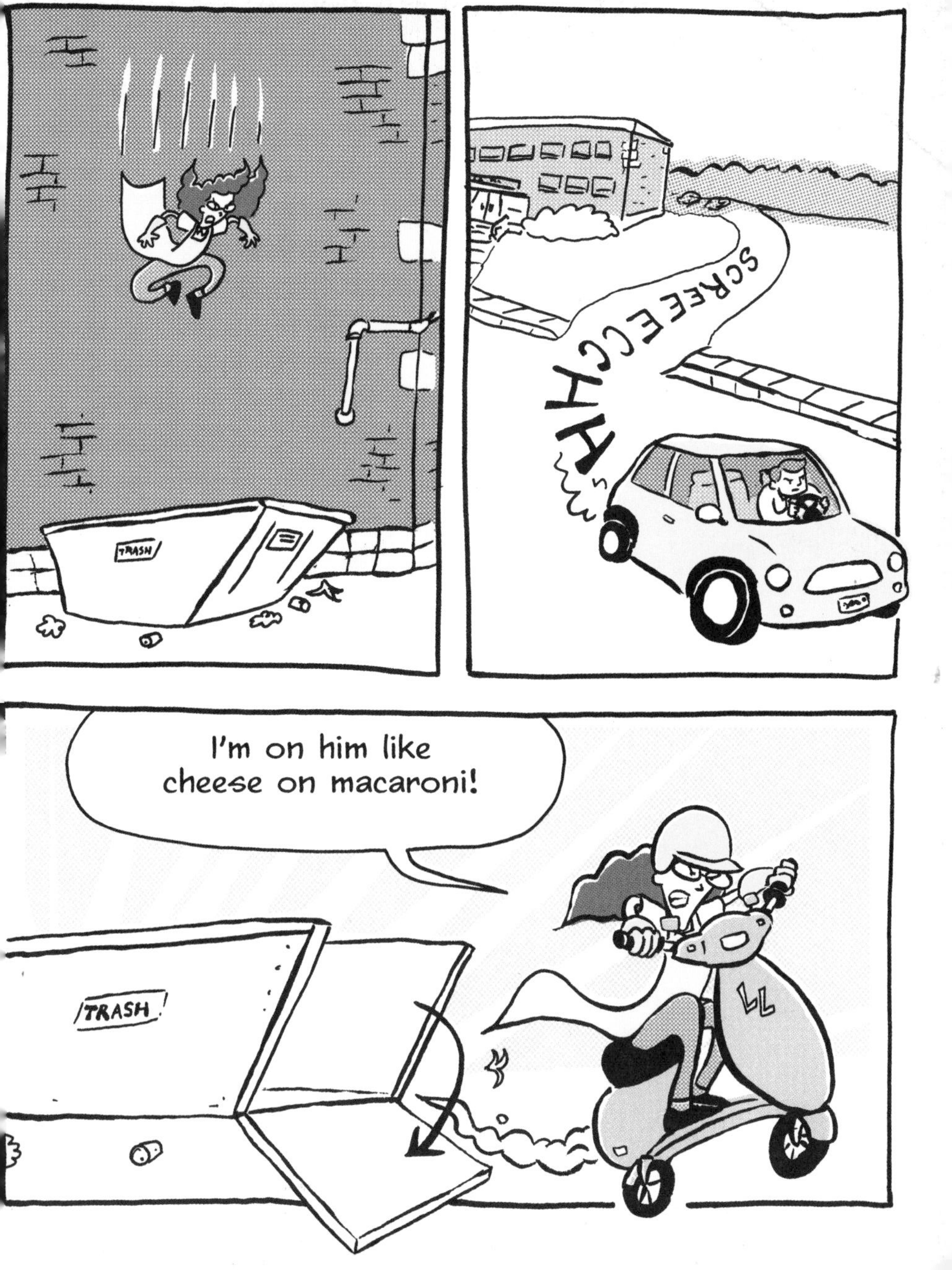
TRASH
SCREEECCHH
I'm on him like cheese on macaroni!
TRASH

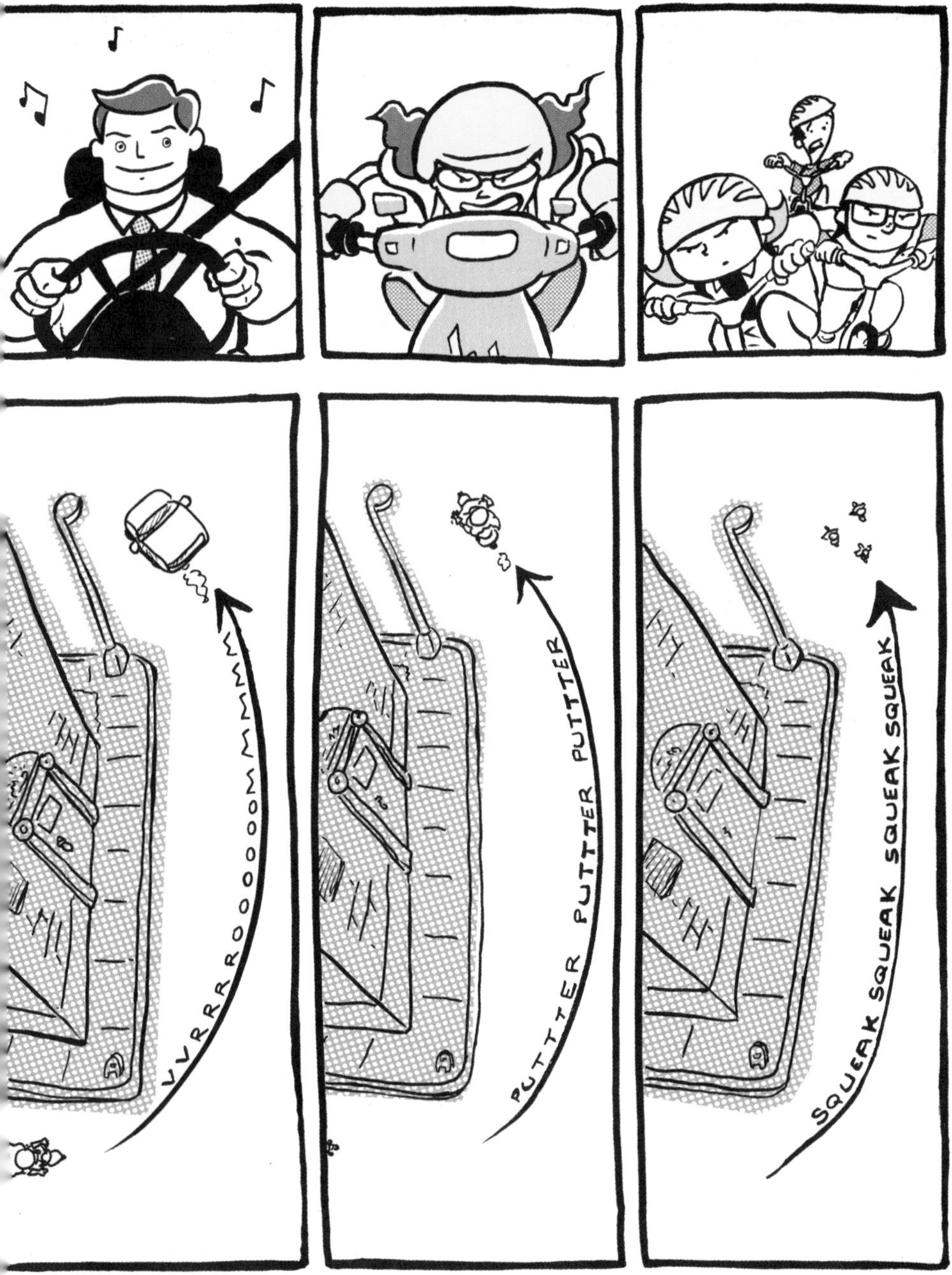
VVRRRROOOOOOOMMMMM
PUTTTER PUTTTER PUTTTER
SQUEAK SQUEAK SQUEAK SQUEAK

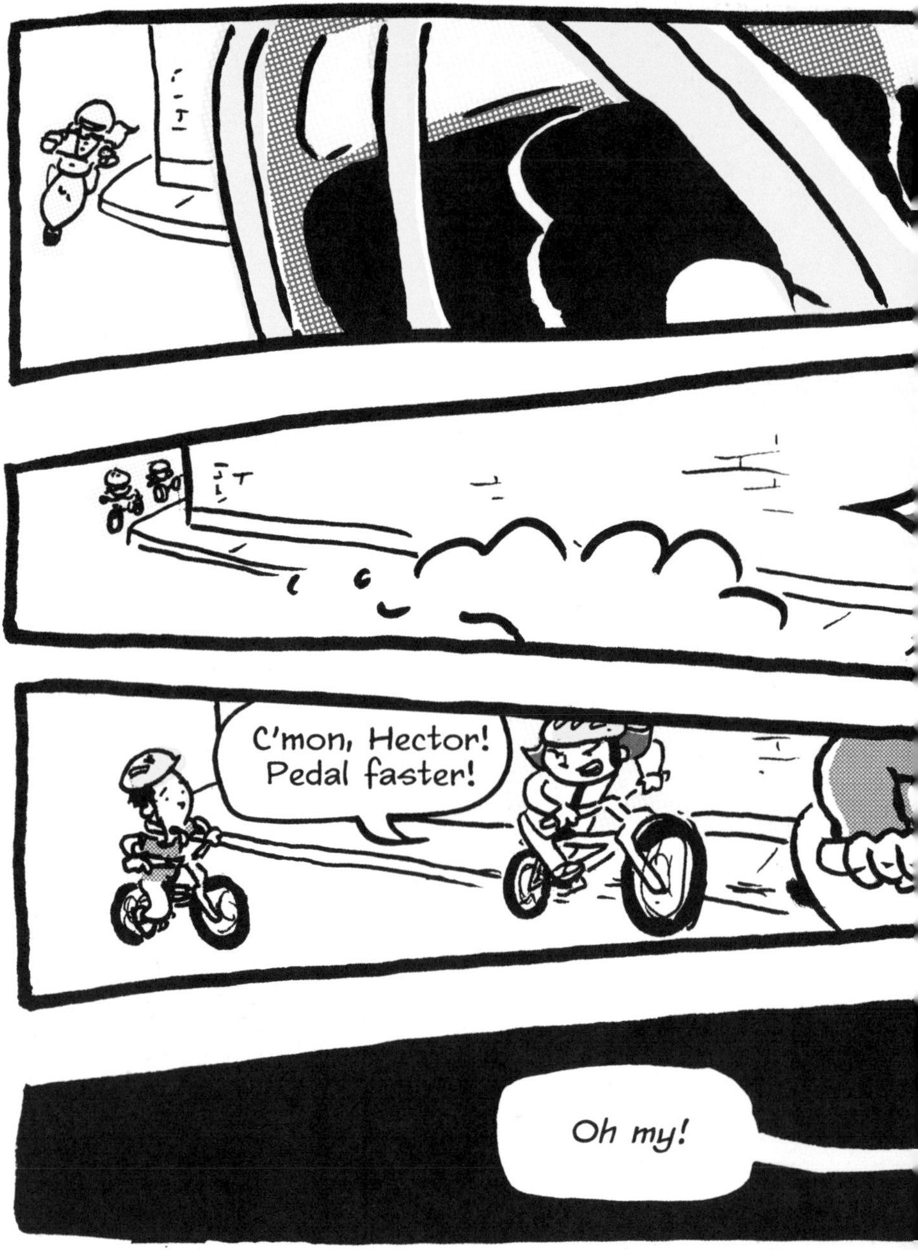
C'mon, Hector! Pedal faster!
Oh my!

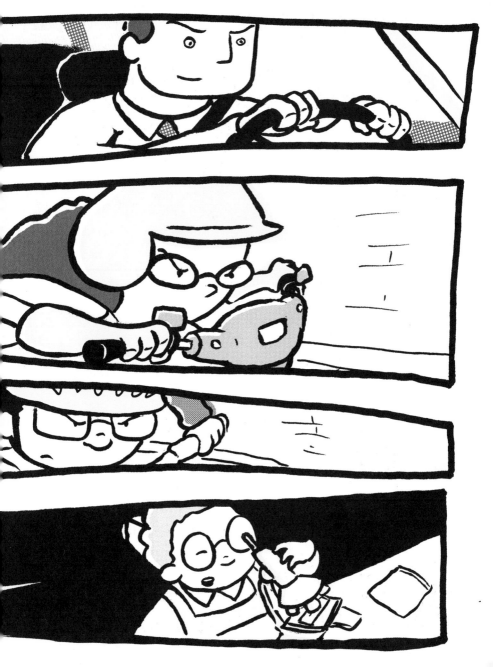

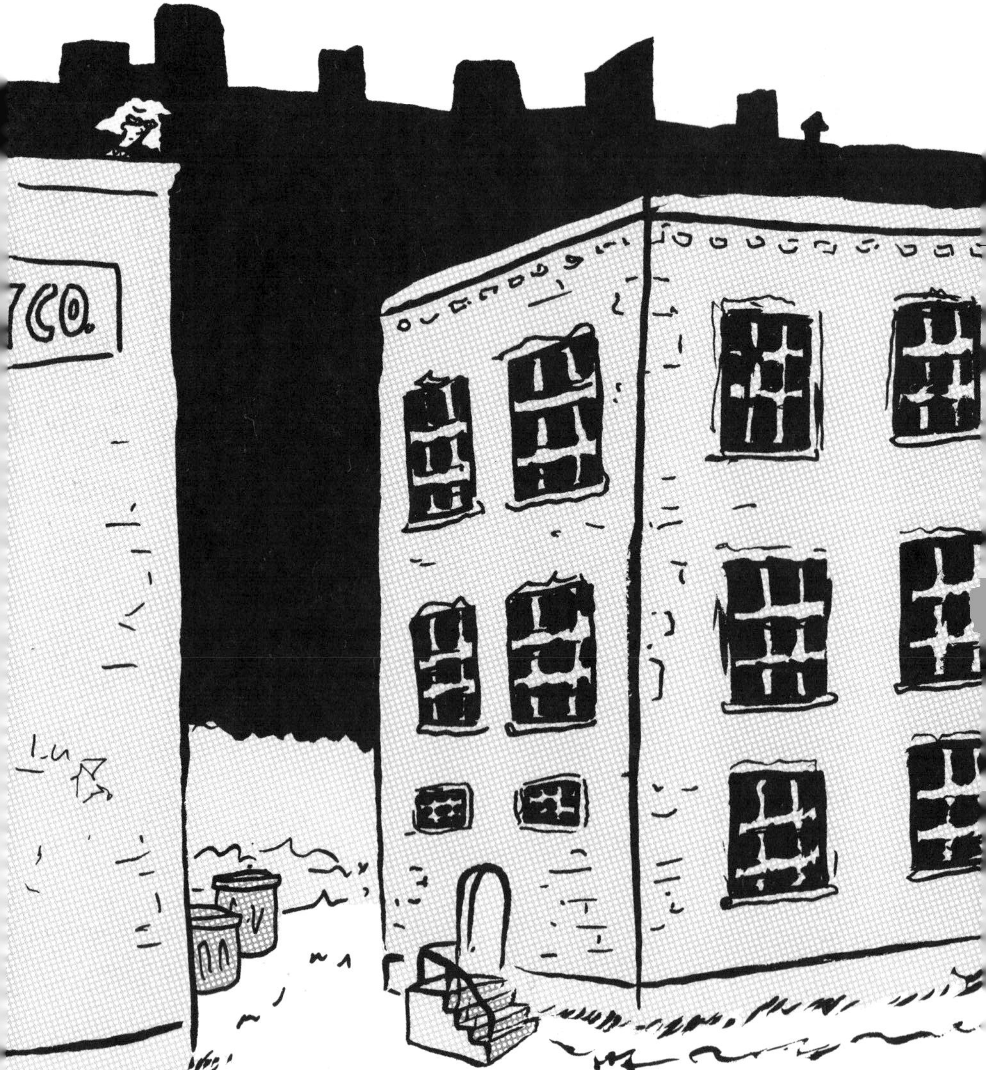
CO.

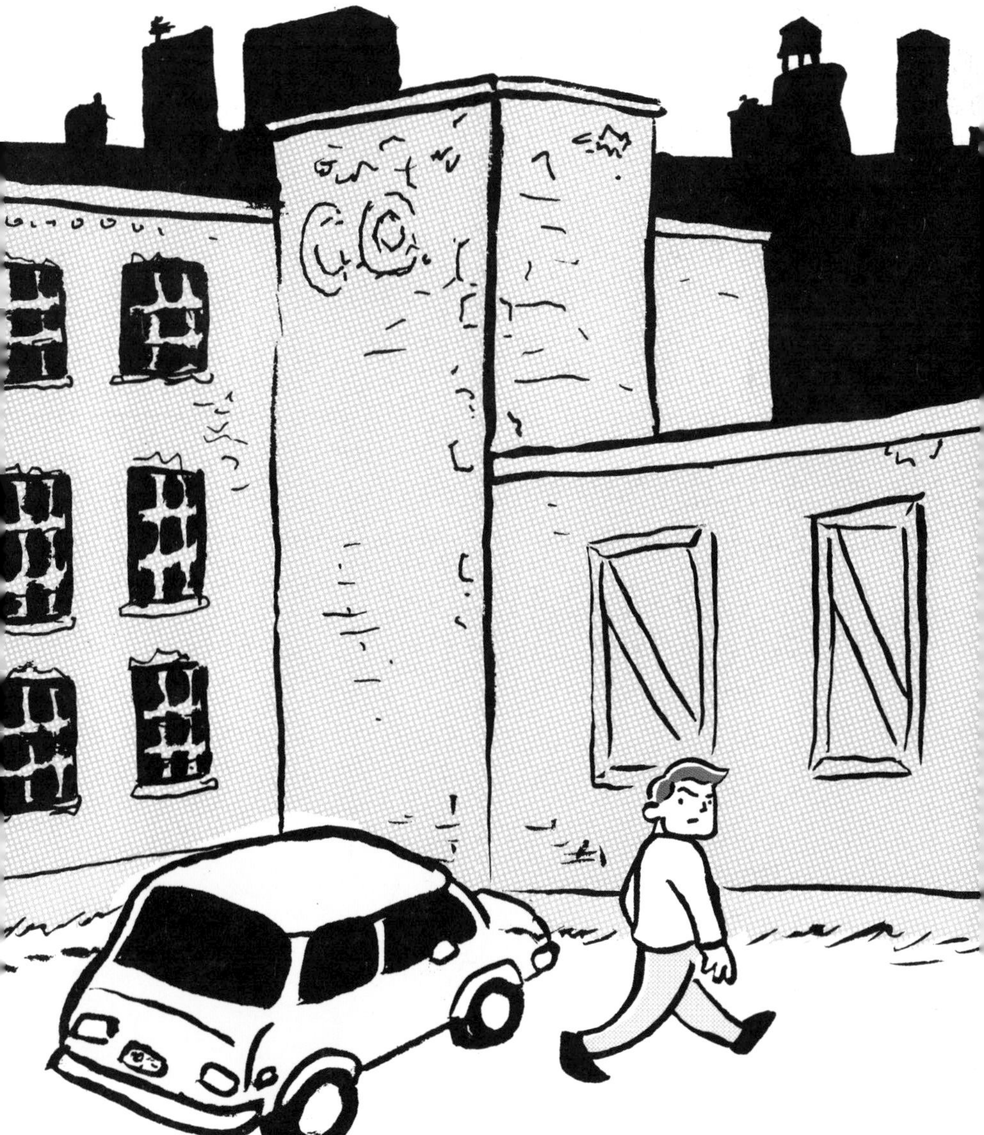

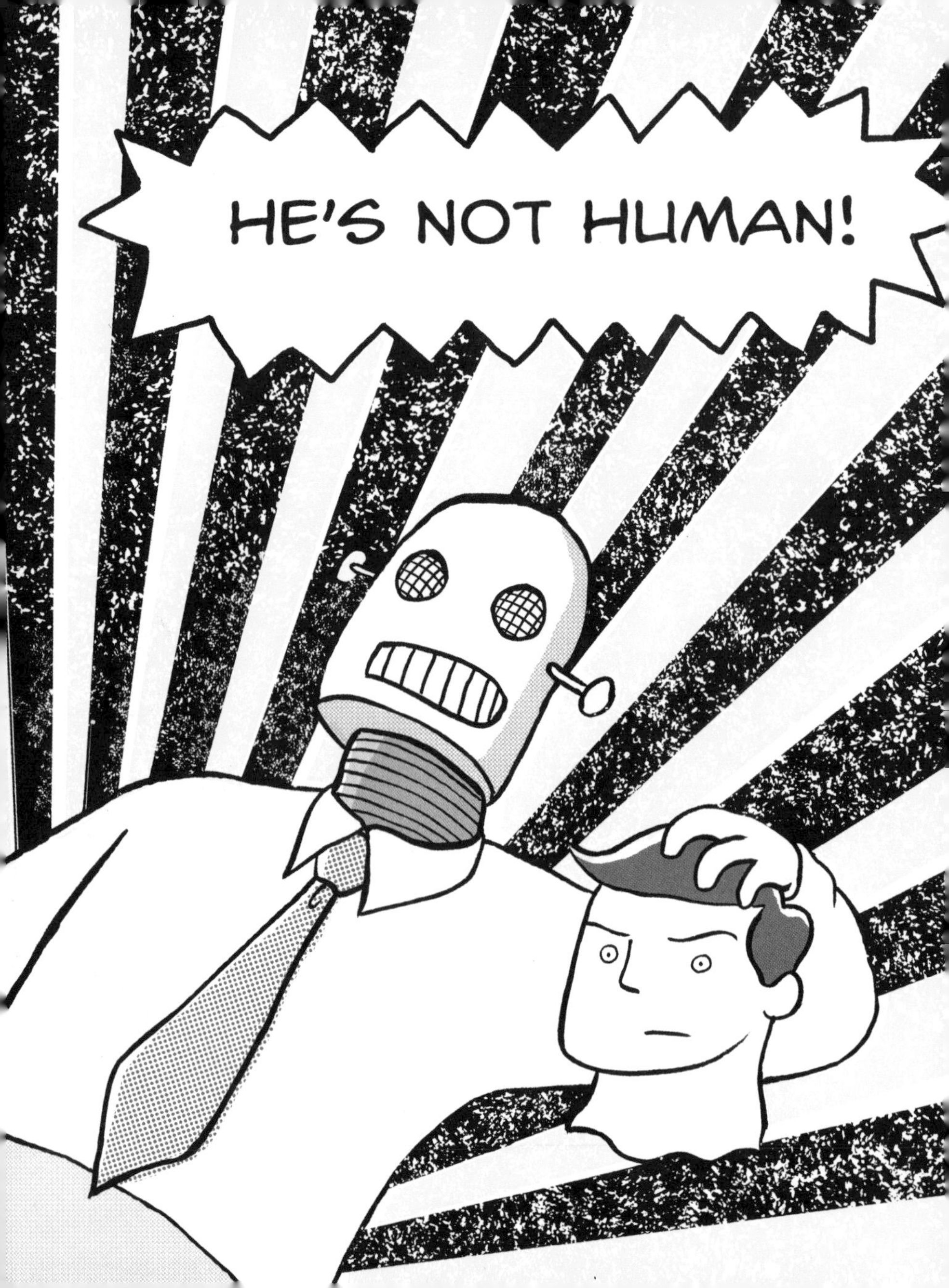
HE'S NOT HUMAN!

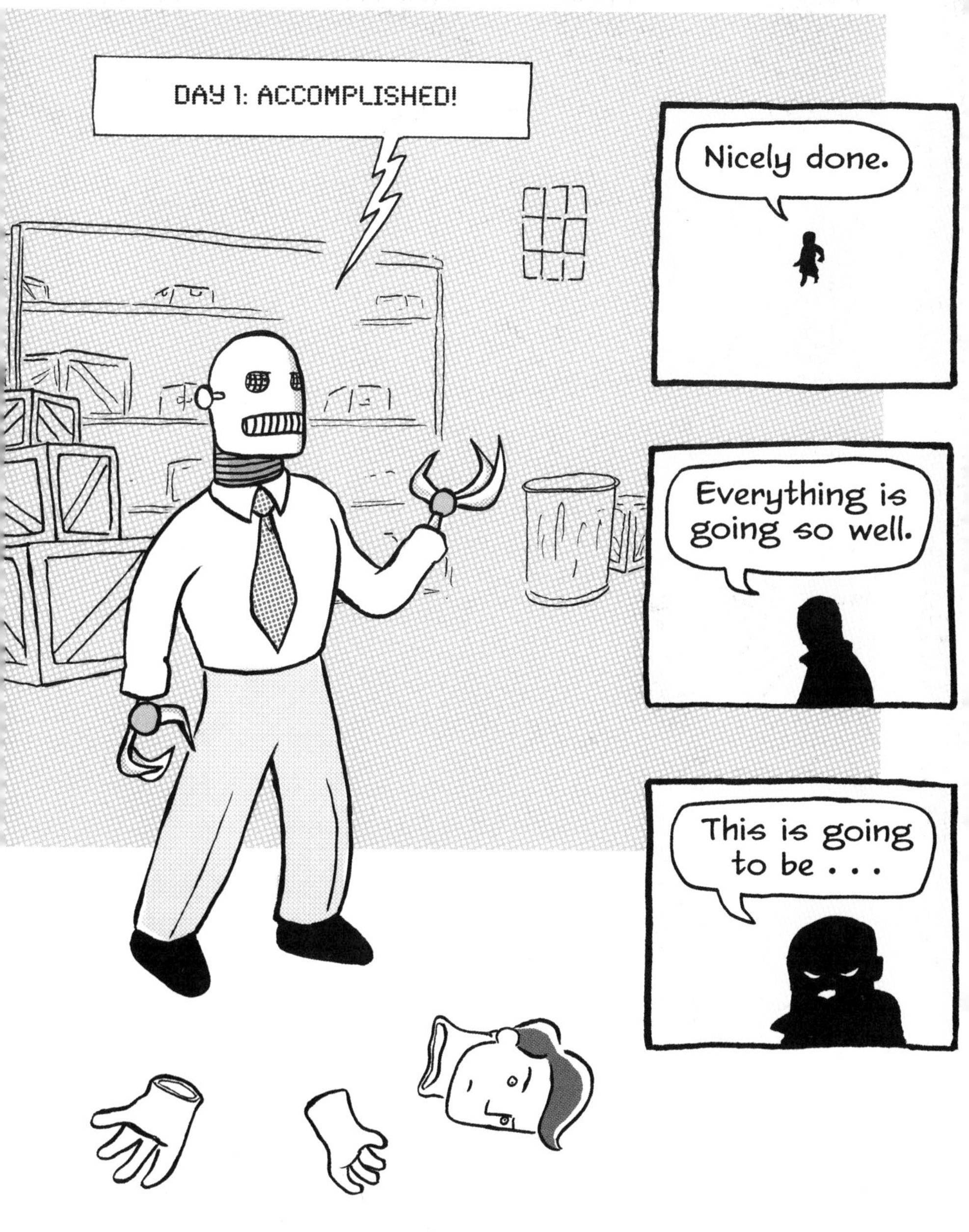
DAY 1: ACCOMPLISHED!
Nicely done.
Everything is going so well.
This is going to be . . .

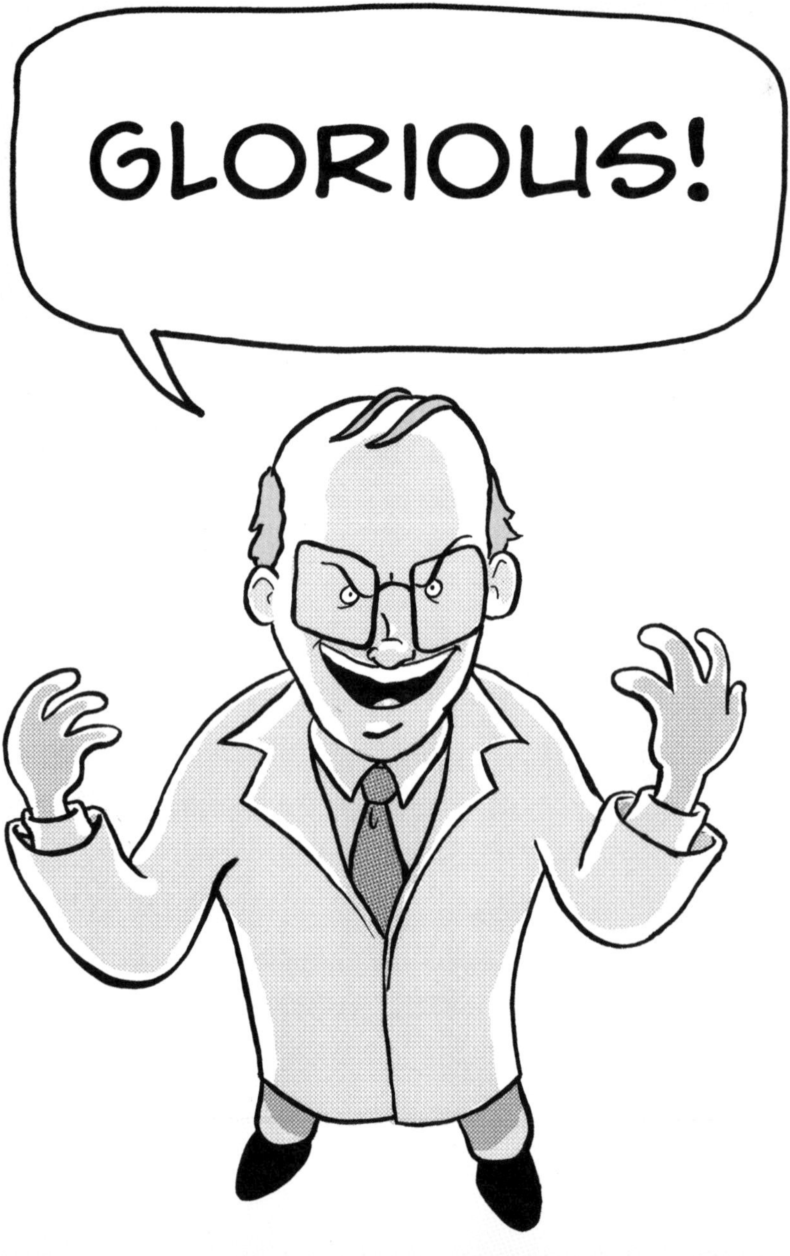
GLORIOUS!

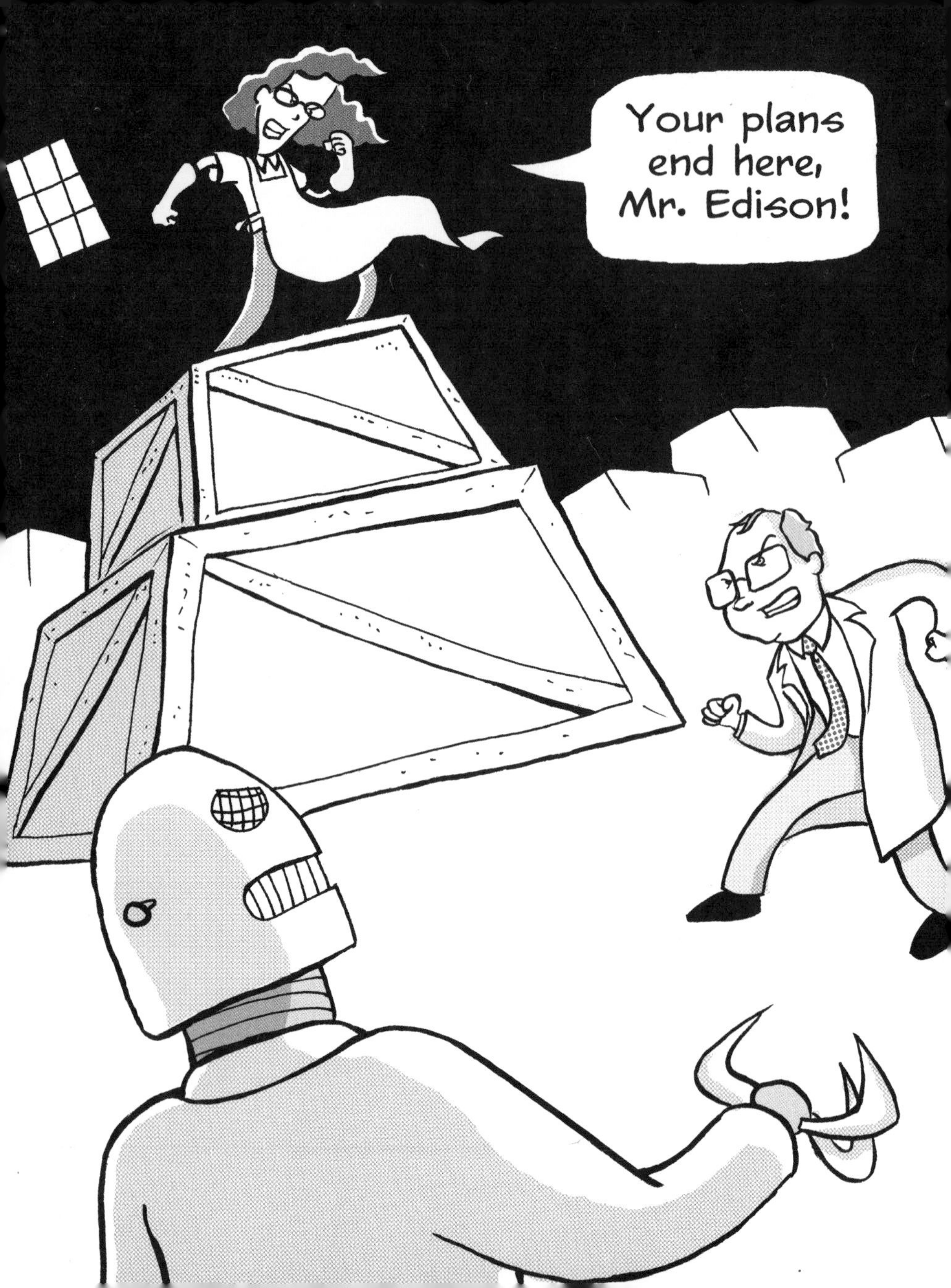
Your plans end here, Mr. Edison!

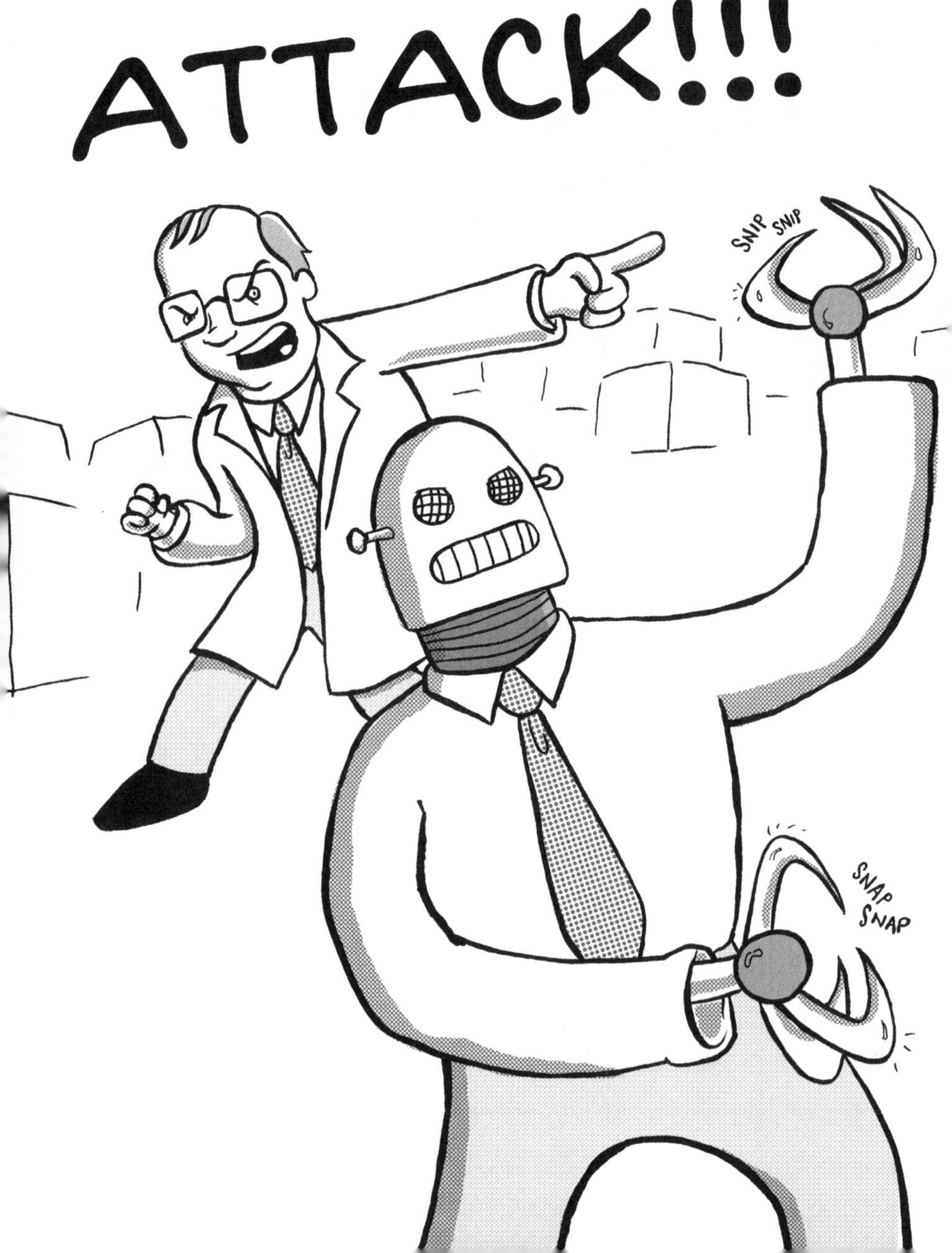
ATTACK!!!
SNIP SNIP
SNAP SNAP

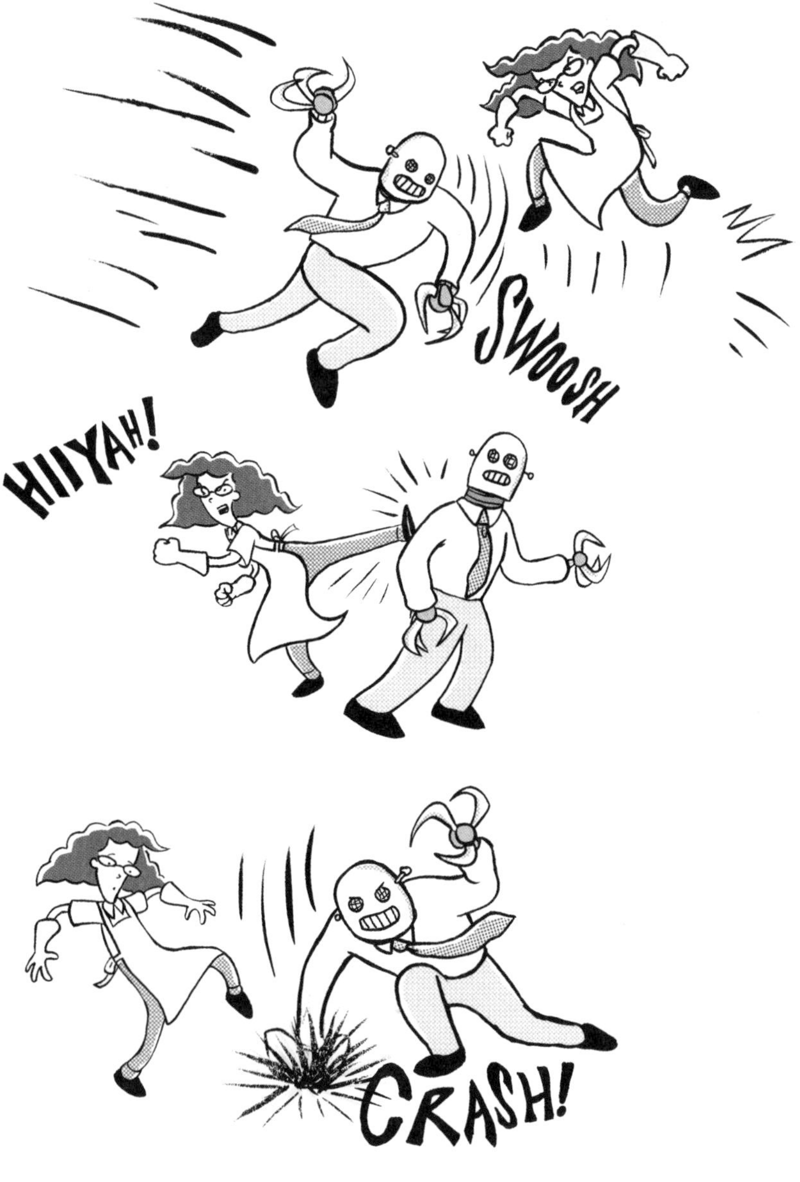
SWOOSH
HIIYAH!
CRASH!

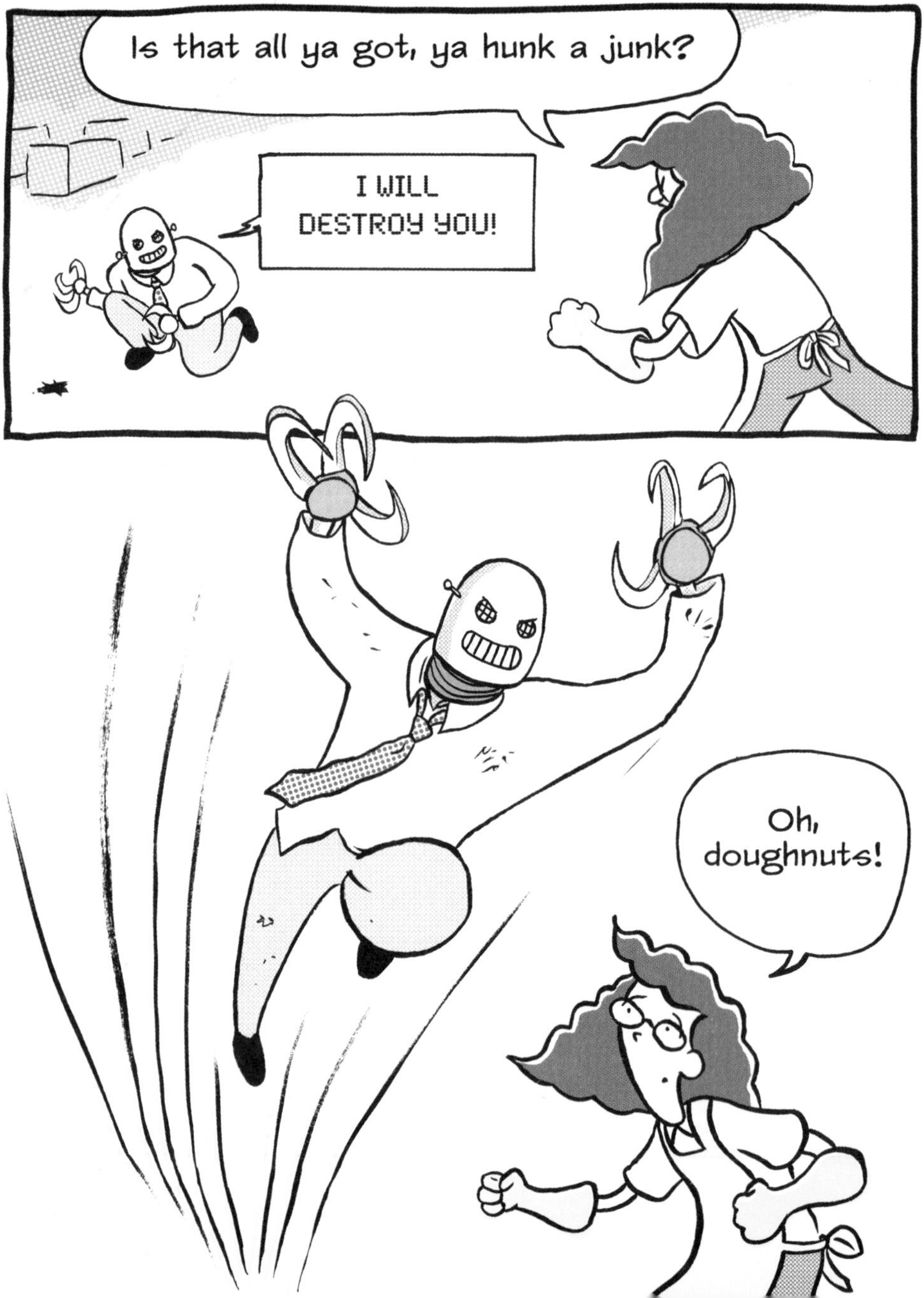
Is that all ya got, ya hunk a junk?
I WILL DESTROY YOU!
Oh, doughnuts!

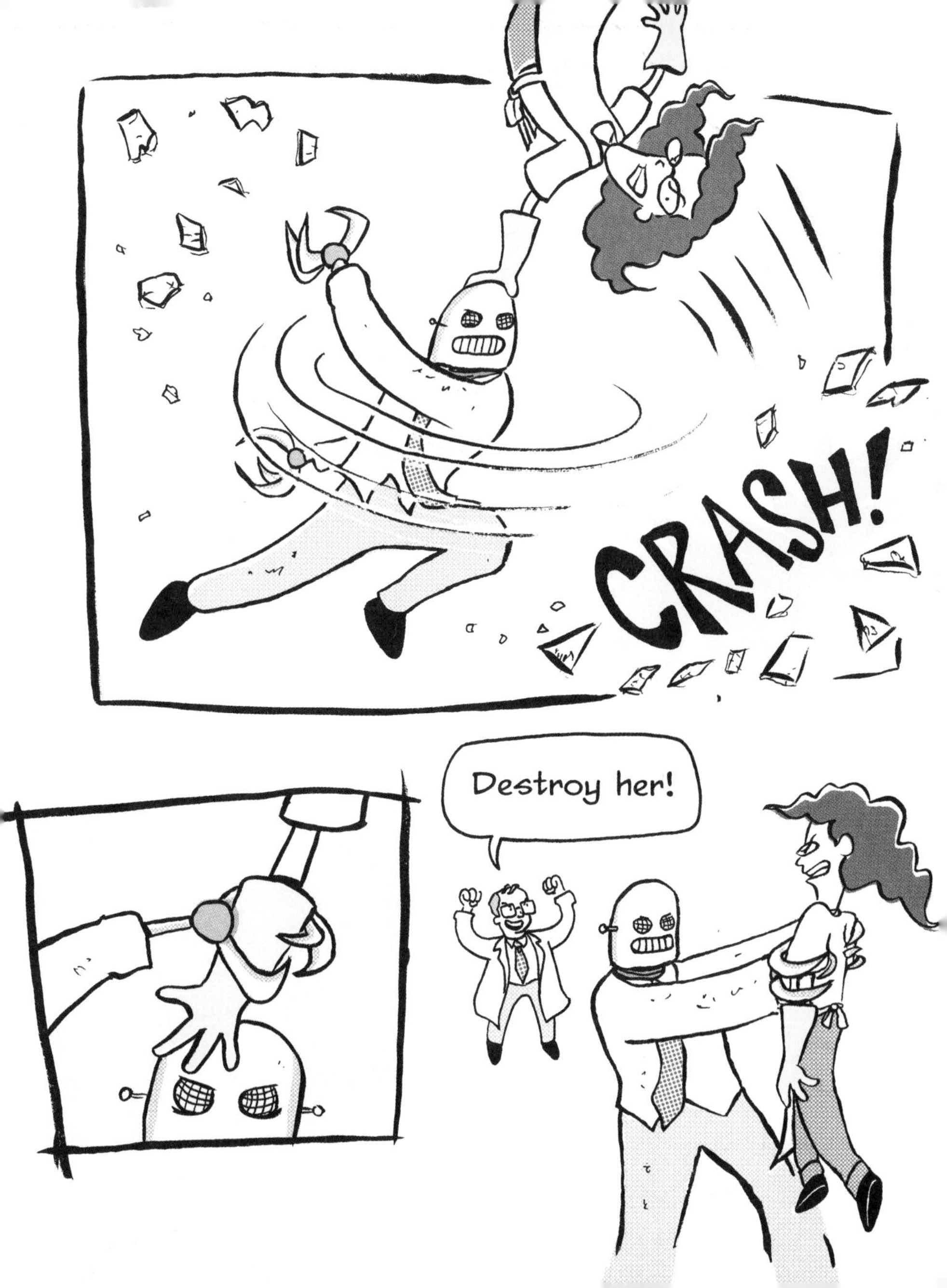
CRASH!
Destroy her!

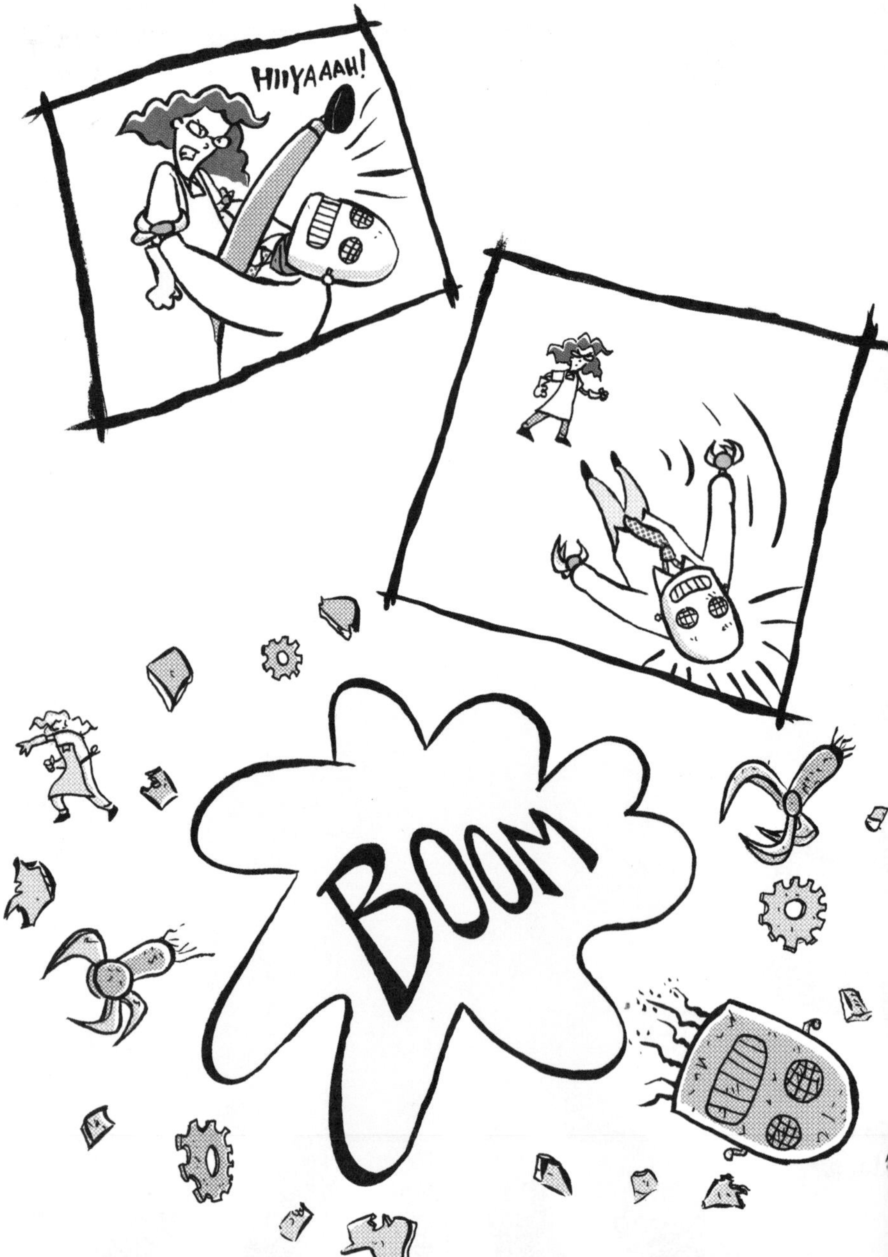
HIIYAAAH!
BOOM

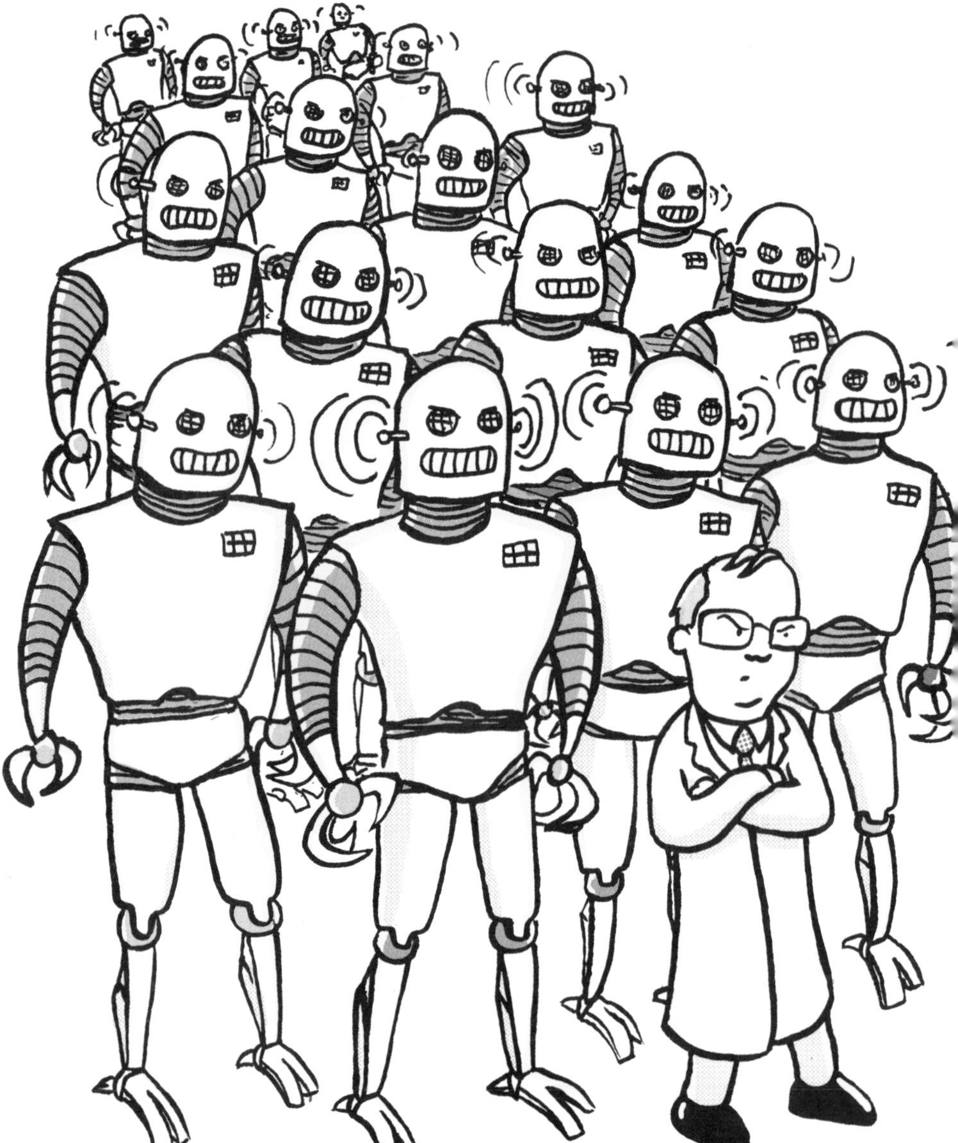

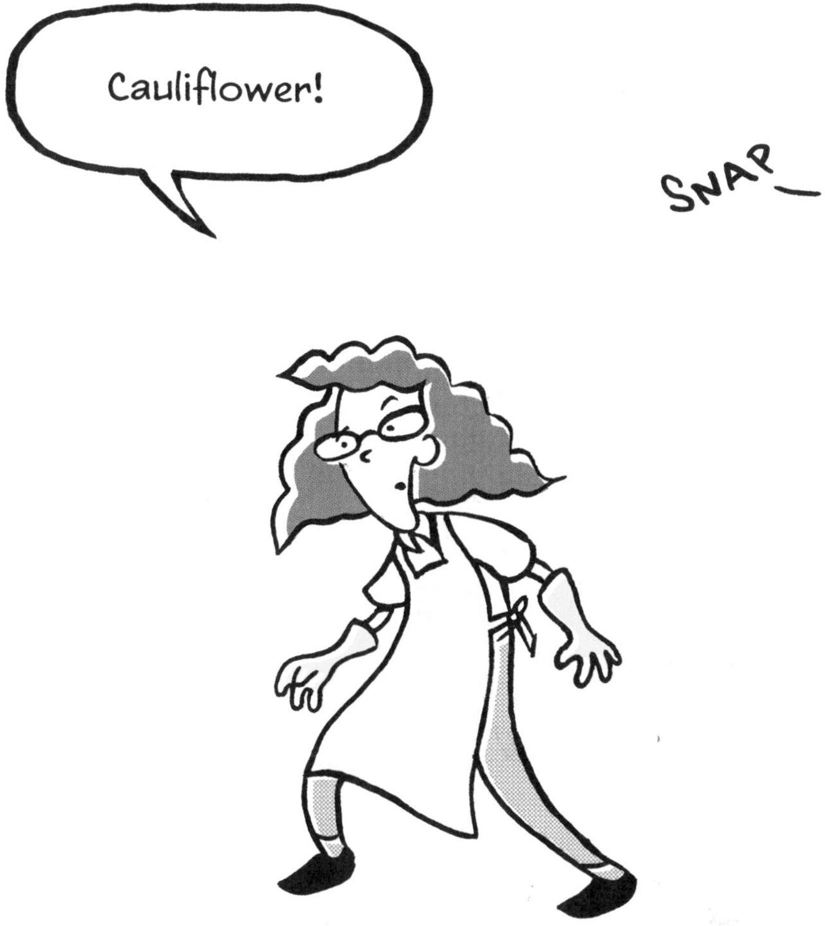
Cauliflower!
SNAP_

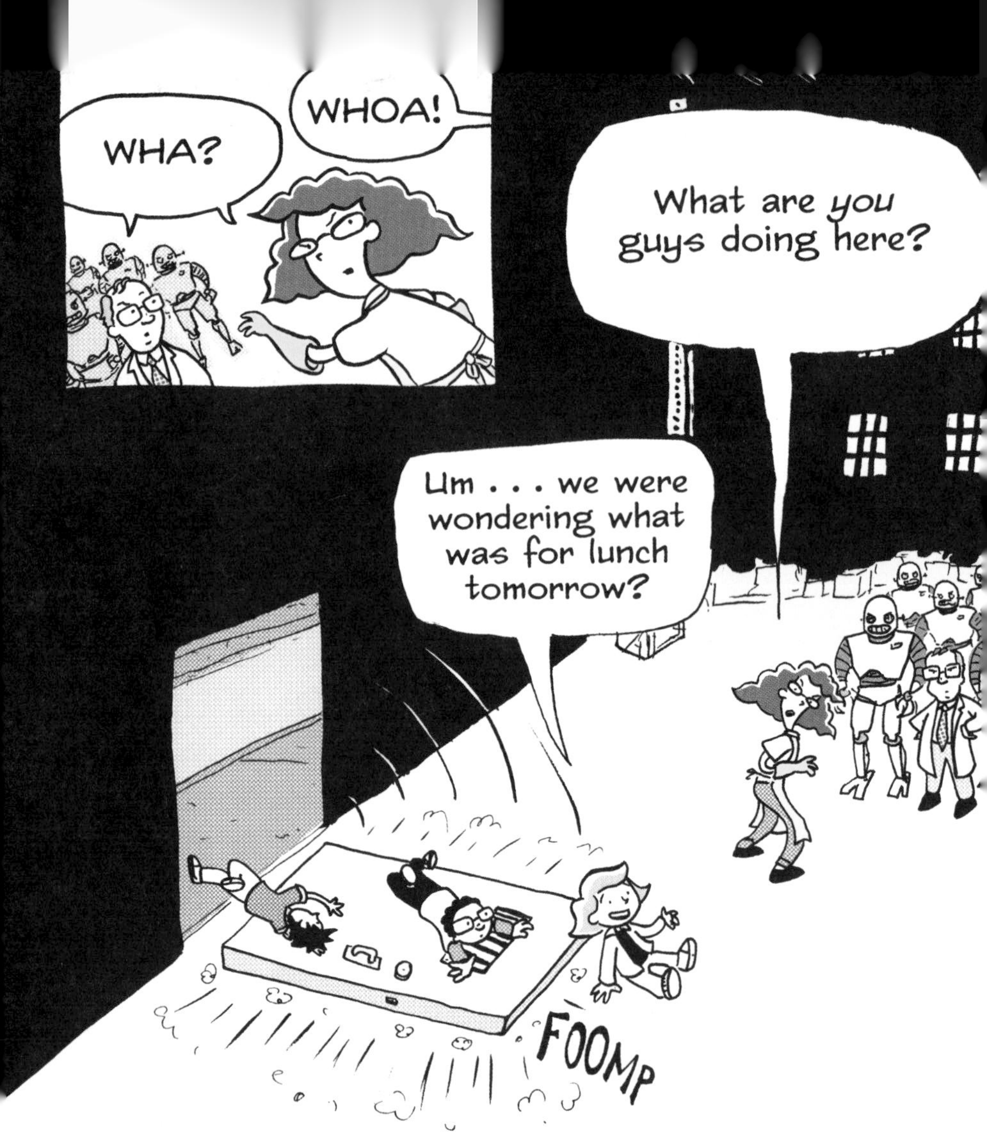
WHA?
WHOA!
What are you guys doing here?
Um . . . we were wondering what was for lunch tomorrow?
FOOMP

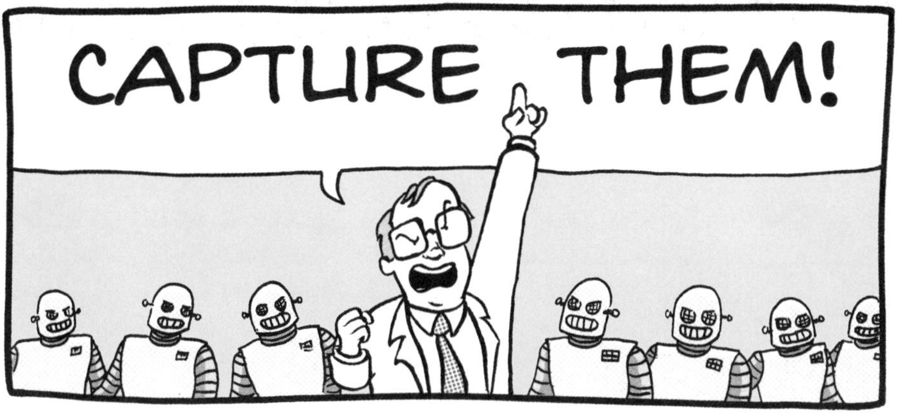
CAPTURE THEM!

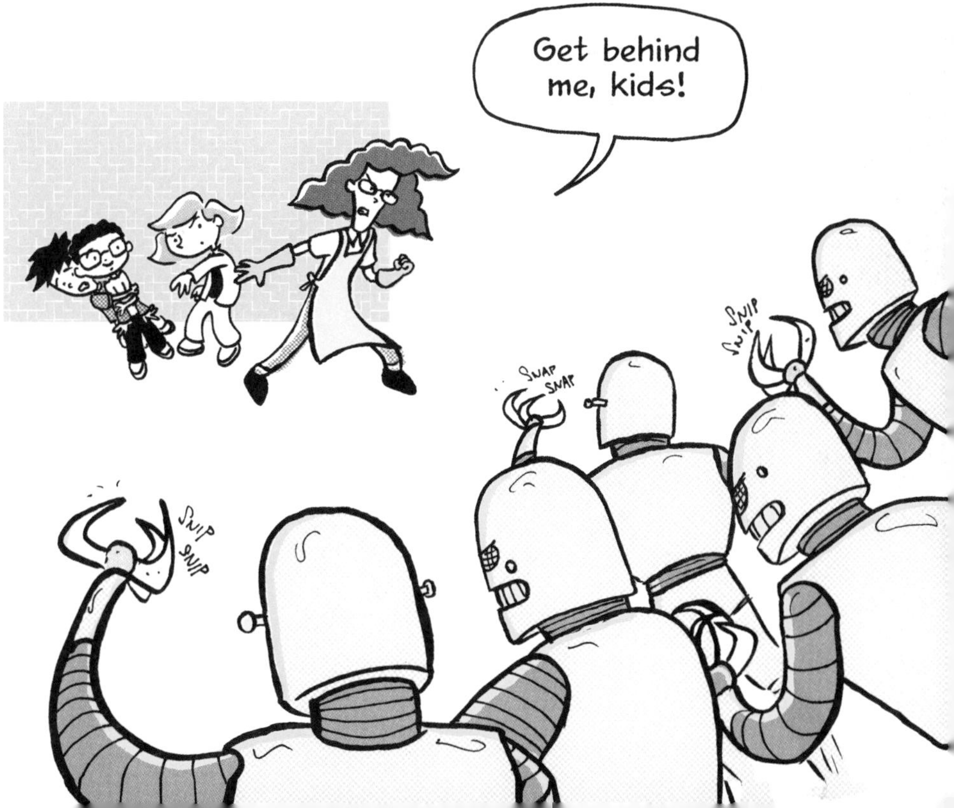
Get behind me, kids!
SNIP SNIP
SNAP SNAP
SNIP SNIP

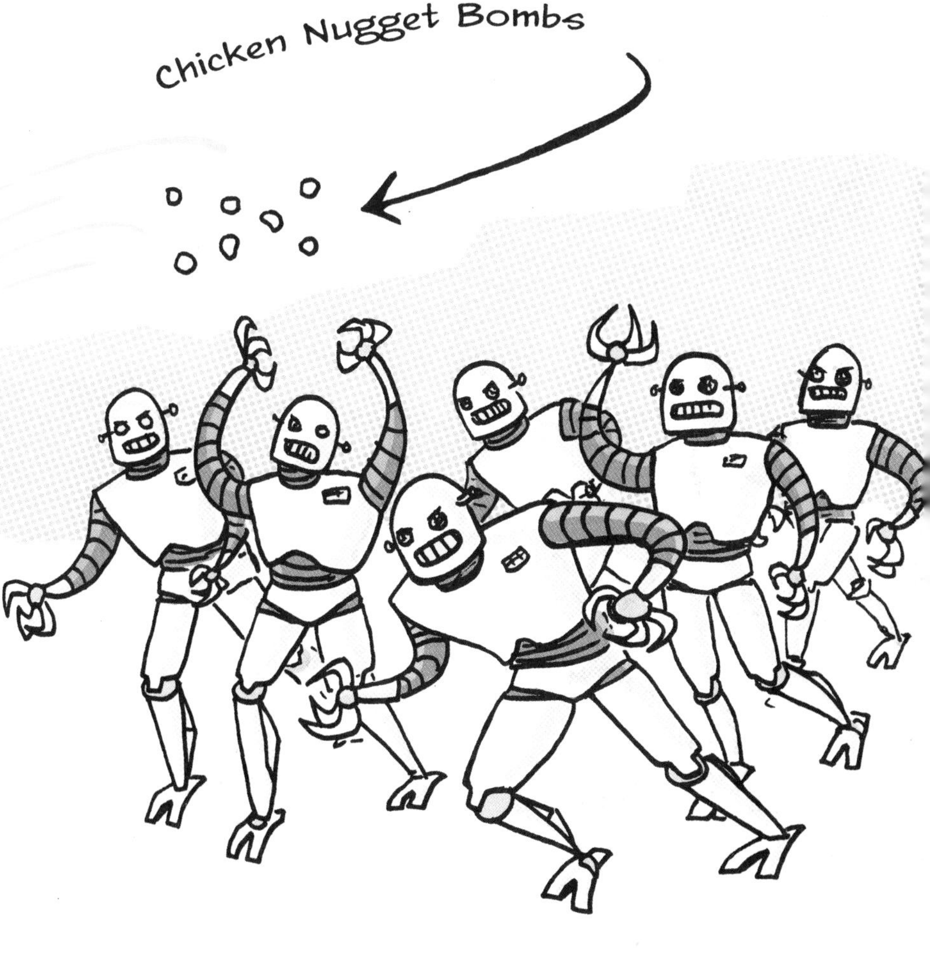
Chicken Nugget Bombs

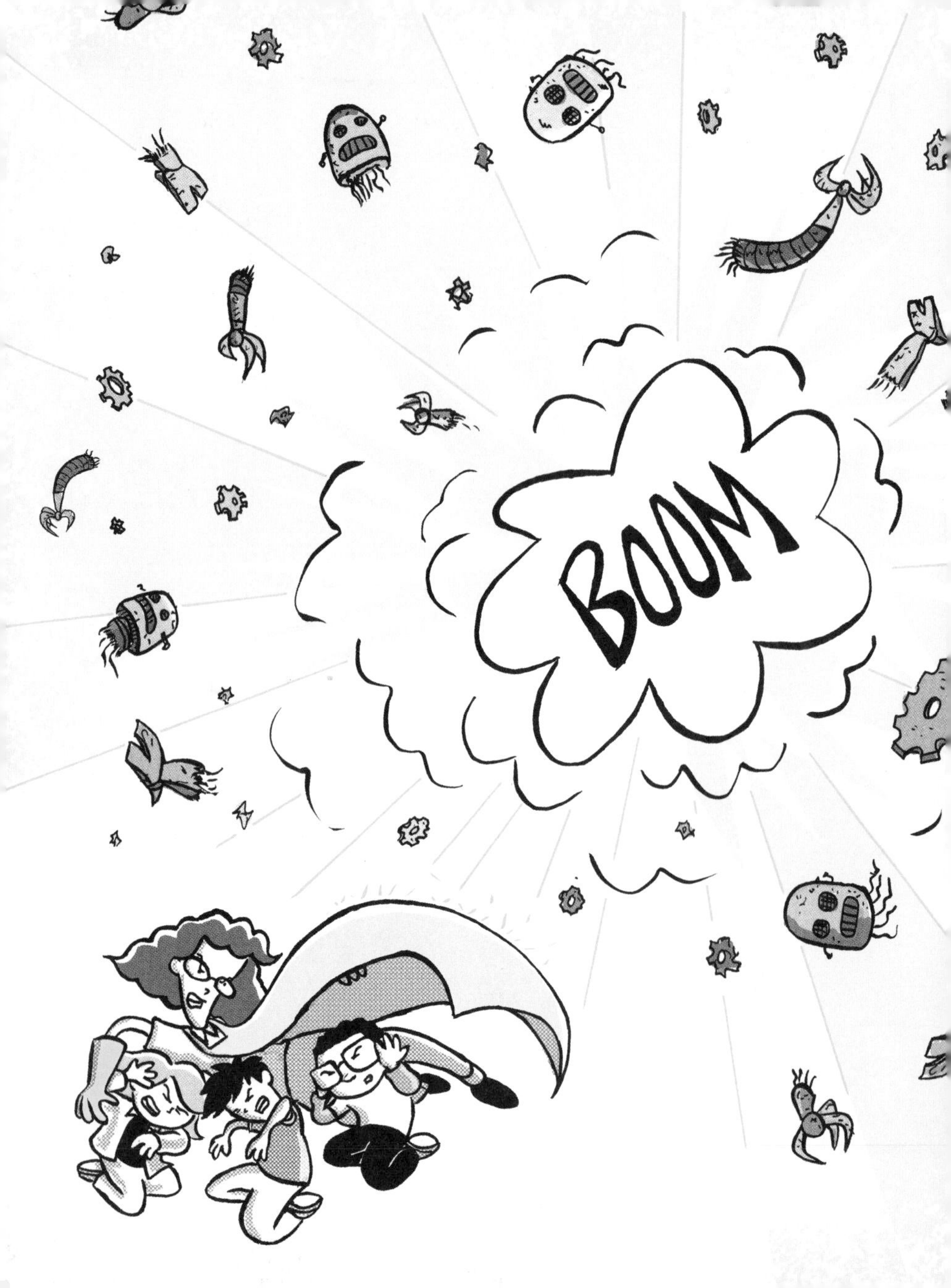
BOOM

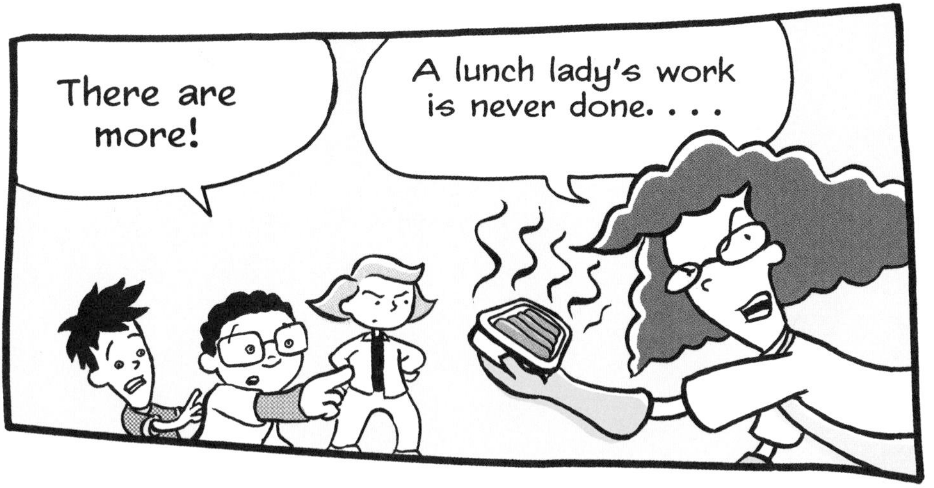
There are more!
A lunch lady's work is never done. . . .

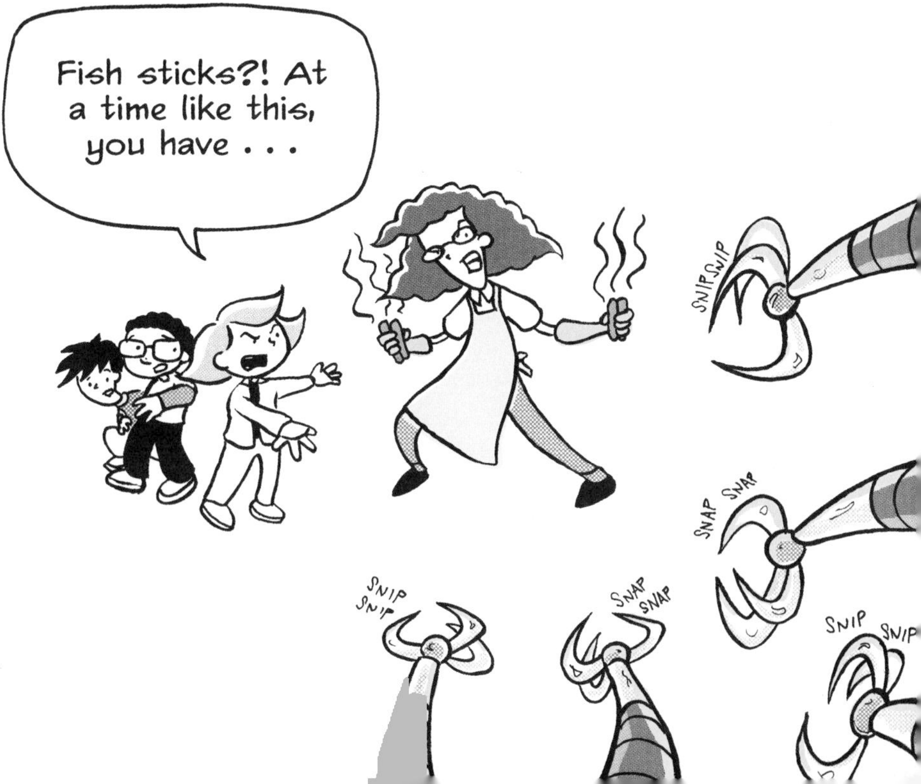
Fish sticks?! At a time like this, you have . . .
SNIP SNIP
SNAP SNAP
SNIP SNIP
SNAP SNAP
SNIP SNIP

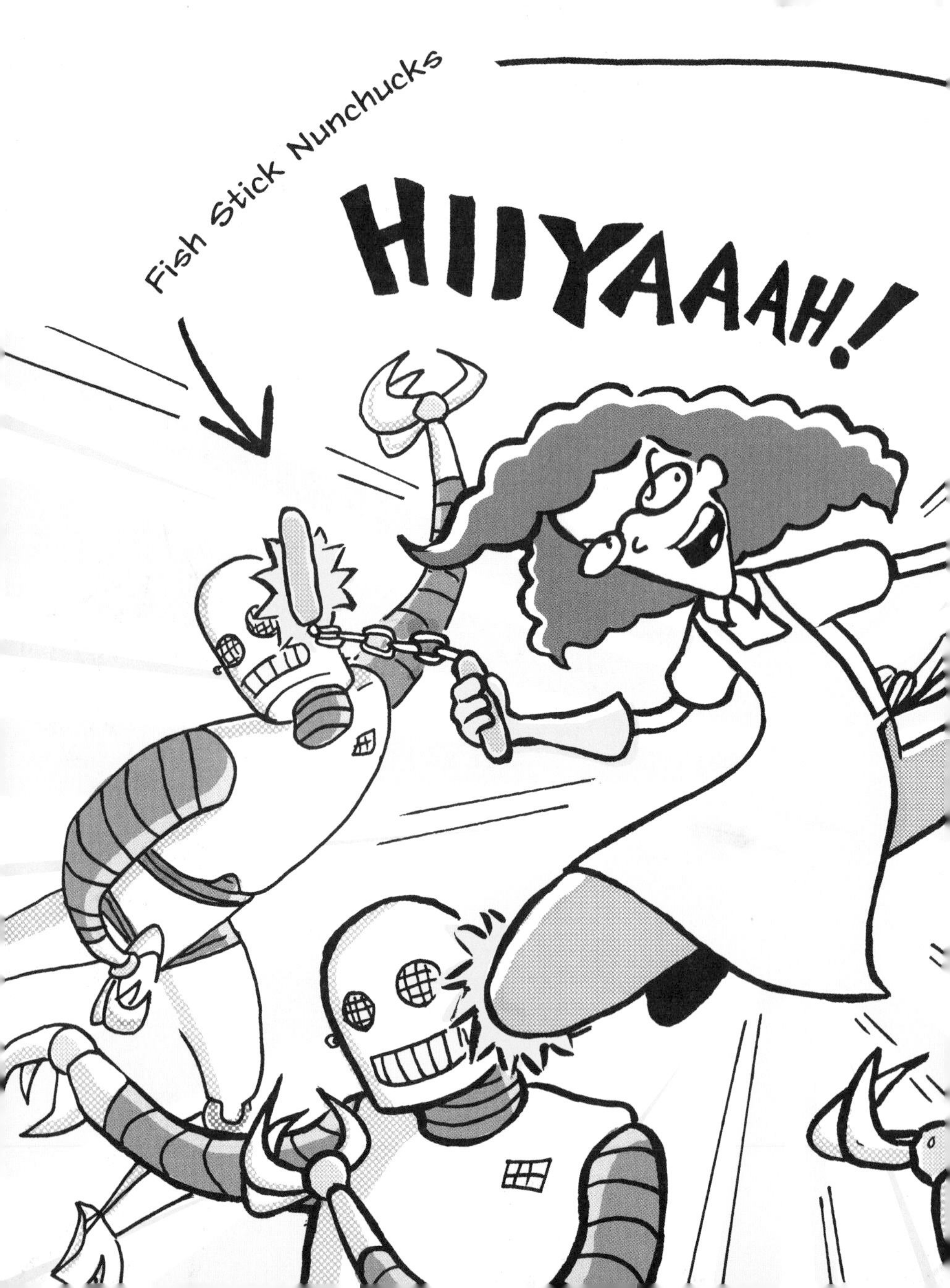

Fish Stick Nunchucks
HIIYAAAAH!

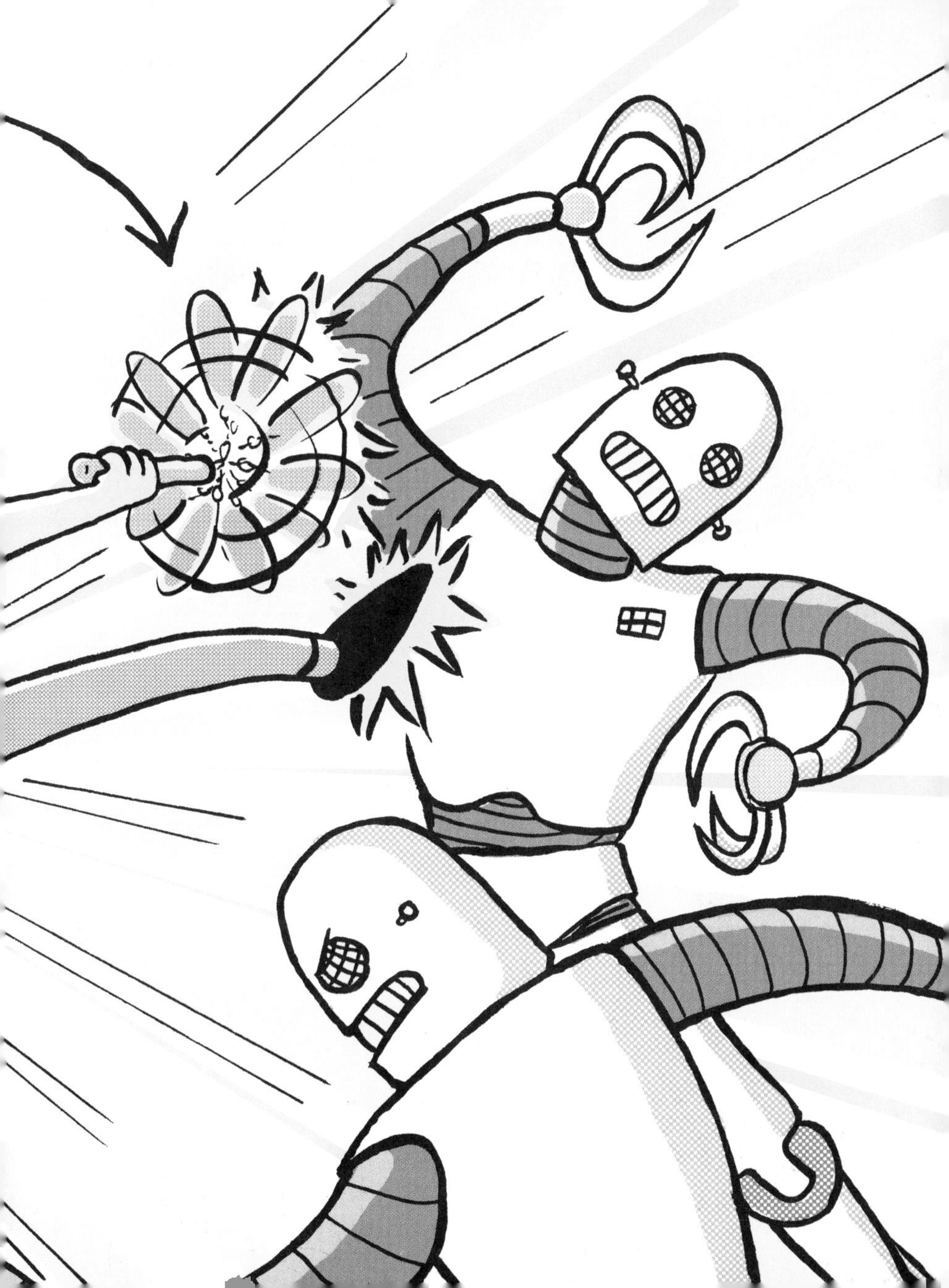

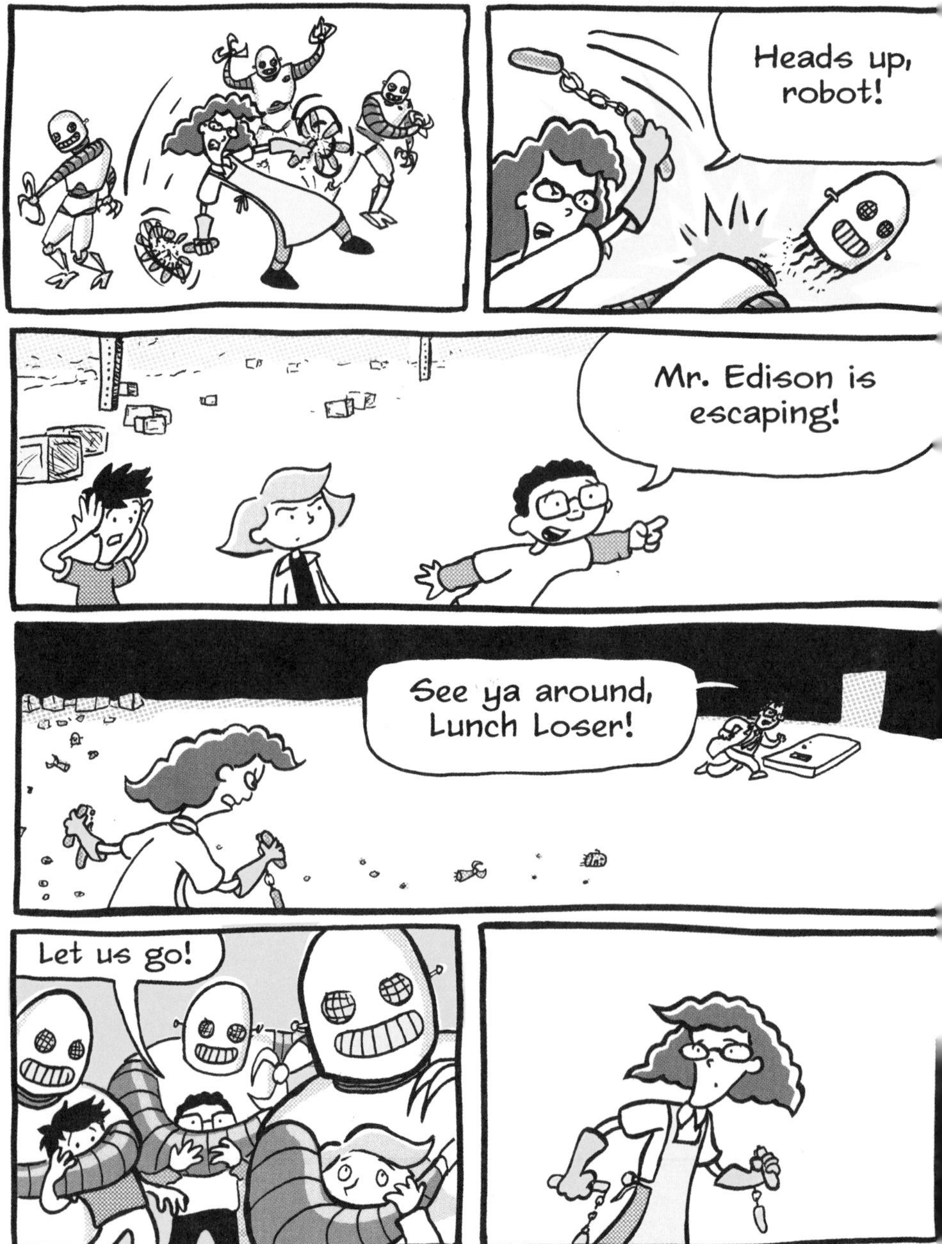
Heads up, robot!
Mr. Edison is escaping!
See ya around, Lunch Loser!
Let us go!

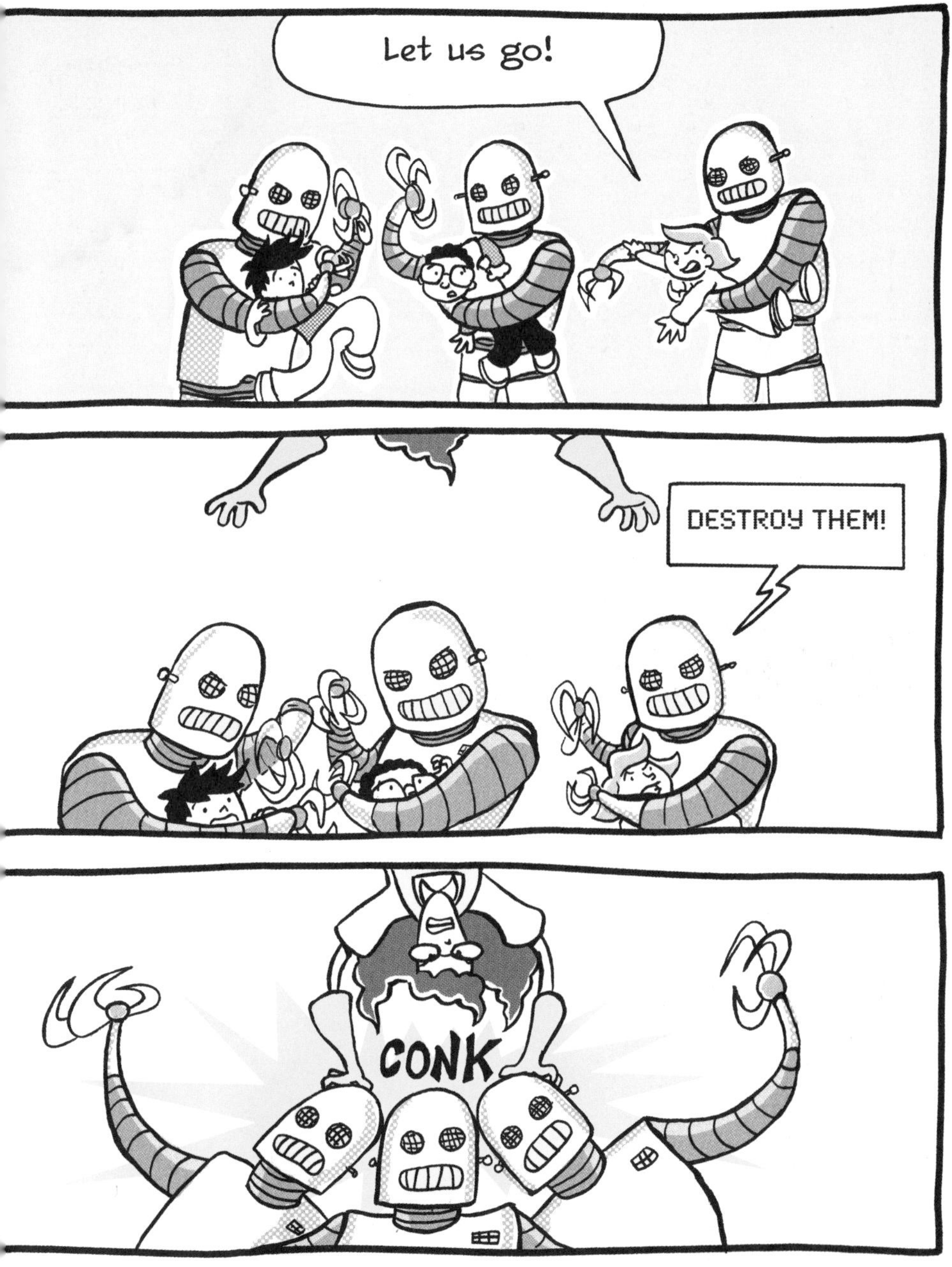
Let us go!
DESTROY THEM!
CONK

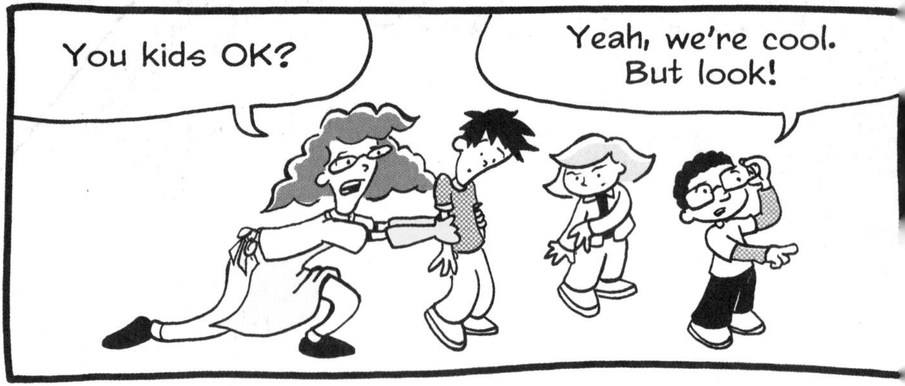
You kids OK?
Yeah, we're cool. But look!

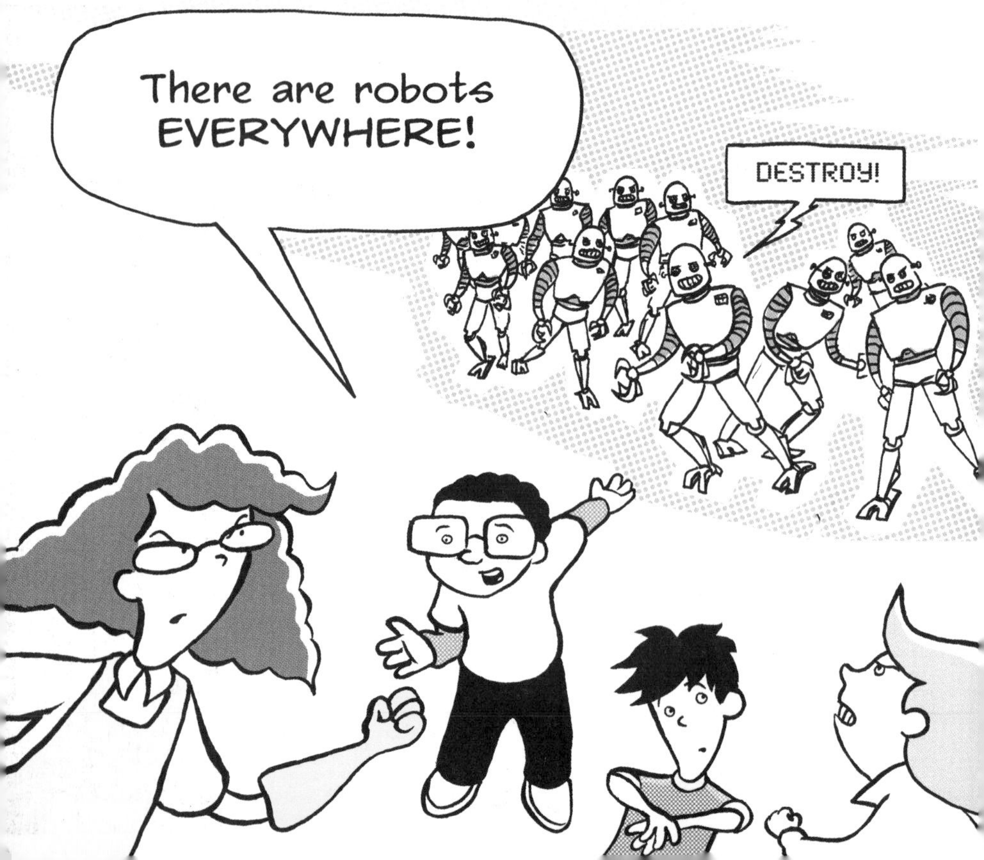
There are robots EVERYWHERE!
DESTROY!

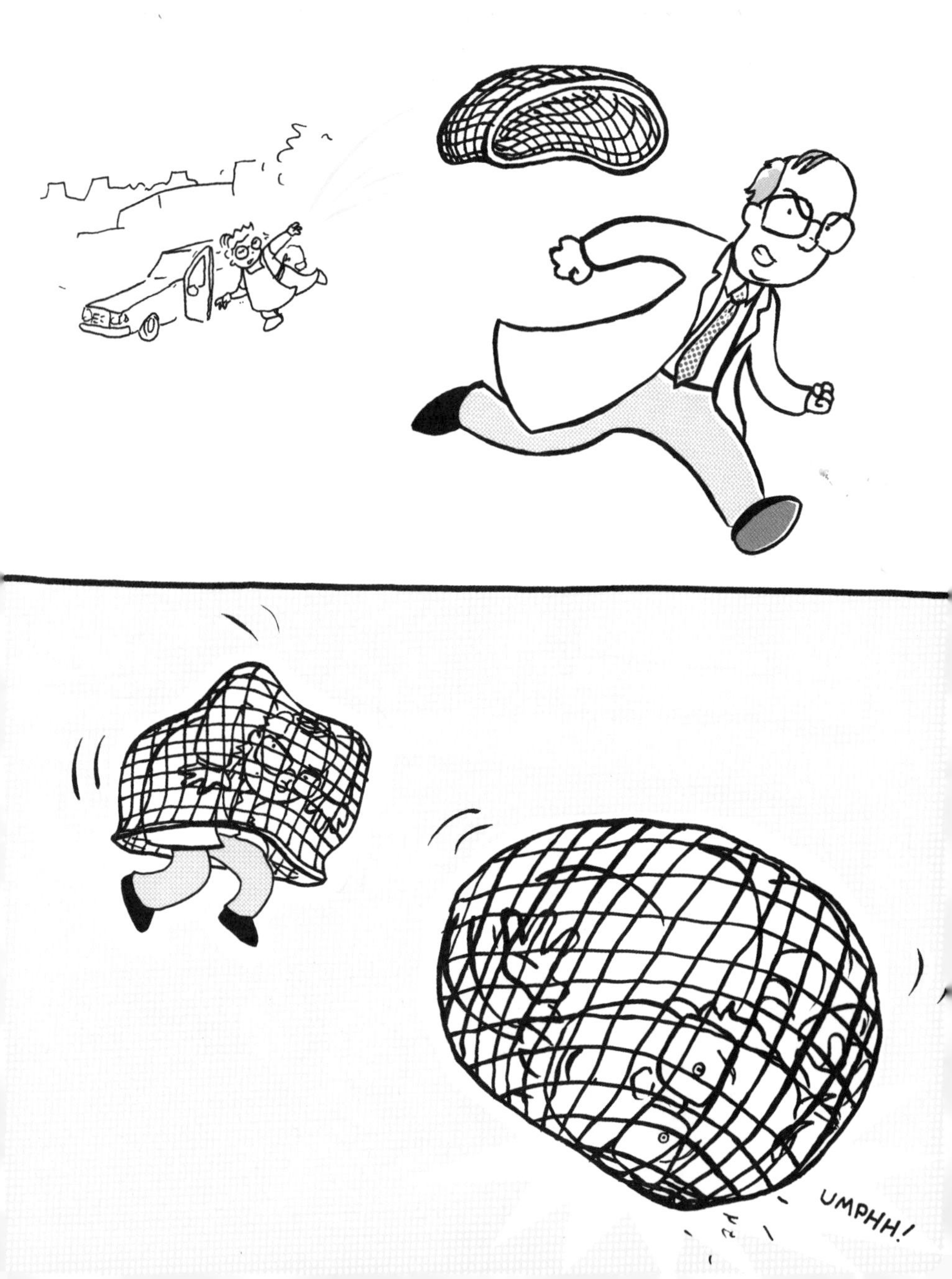
UMPHH!

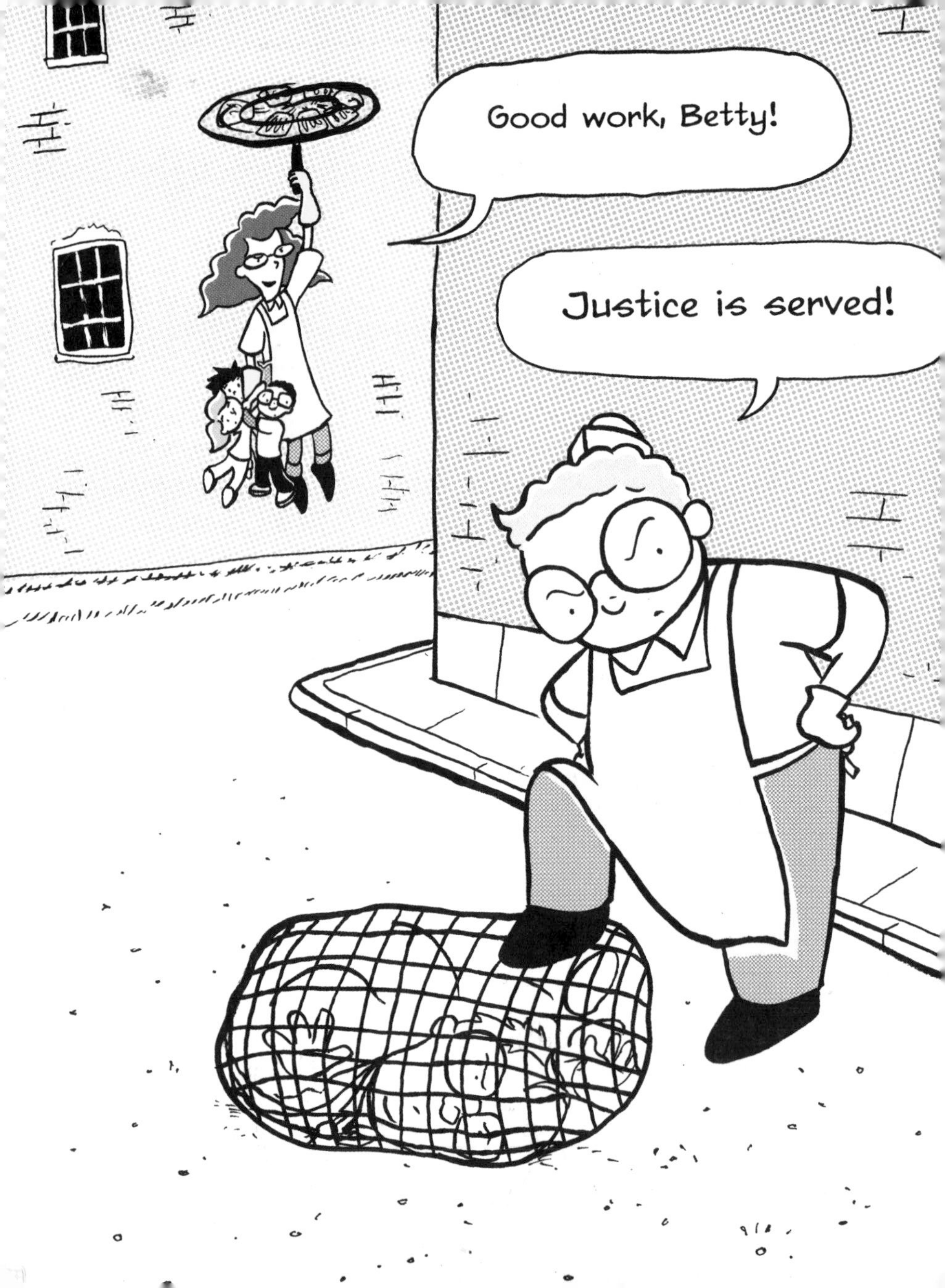
Good work, Betty!
Justice is served!

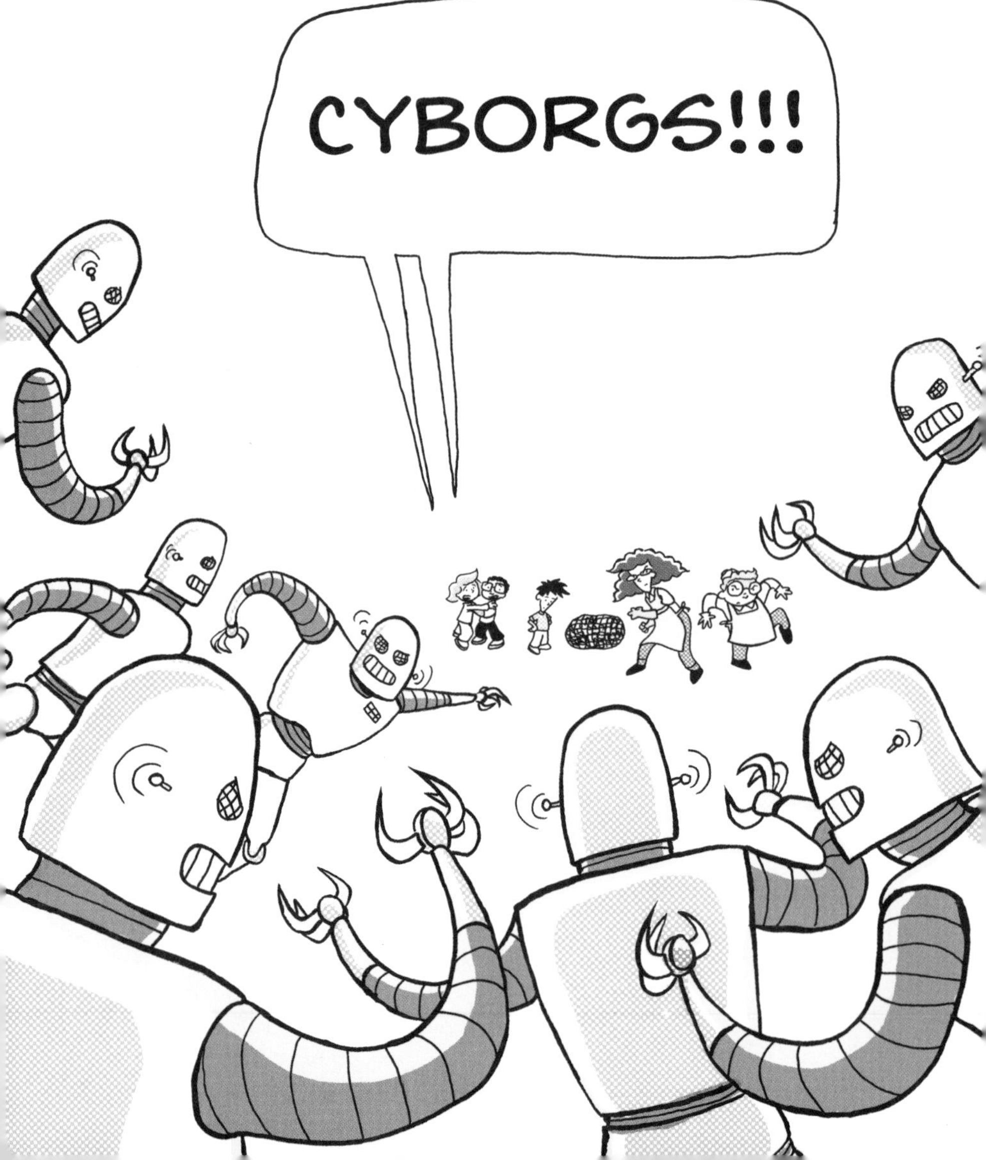
CYBORGS!!!

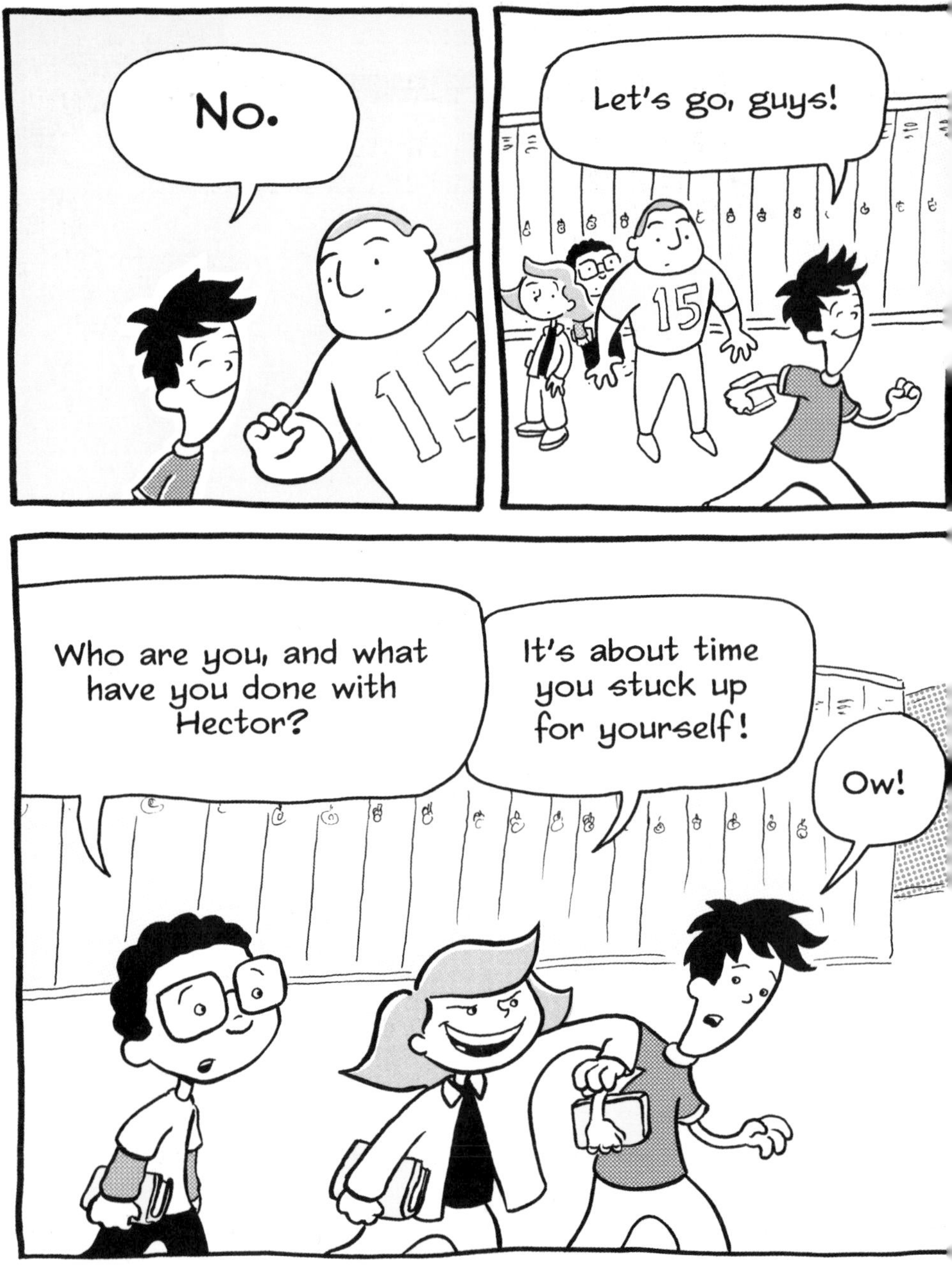
No.
Let's go, guys!
15
Who are you, and what have you done with Hector?
It's about time you stuck up for yourself!
Ow!

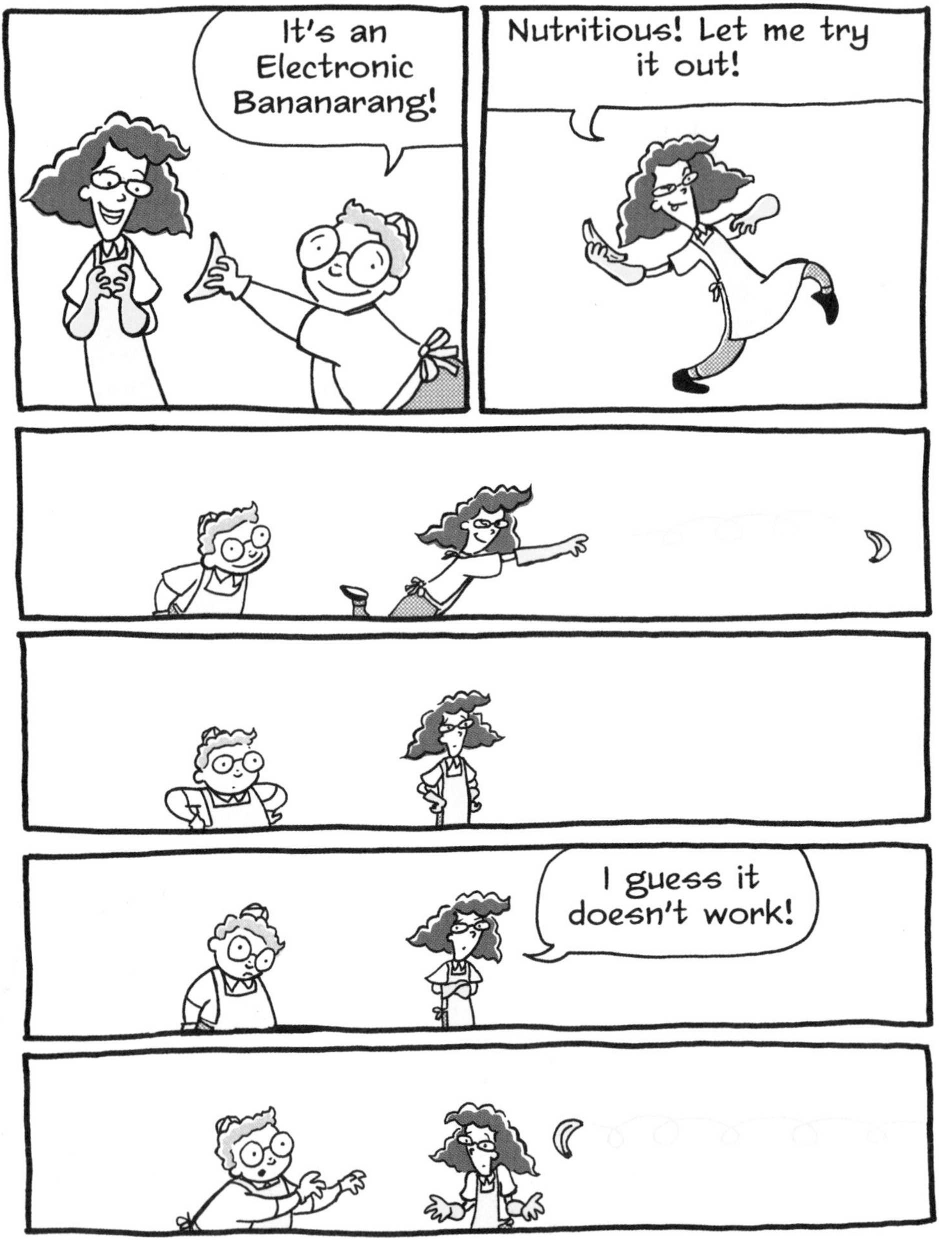
It's an Electronic Bananarang!
Nutritious! Let me try it out!
I guess it doesn't work!

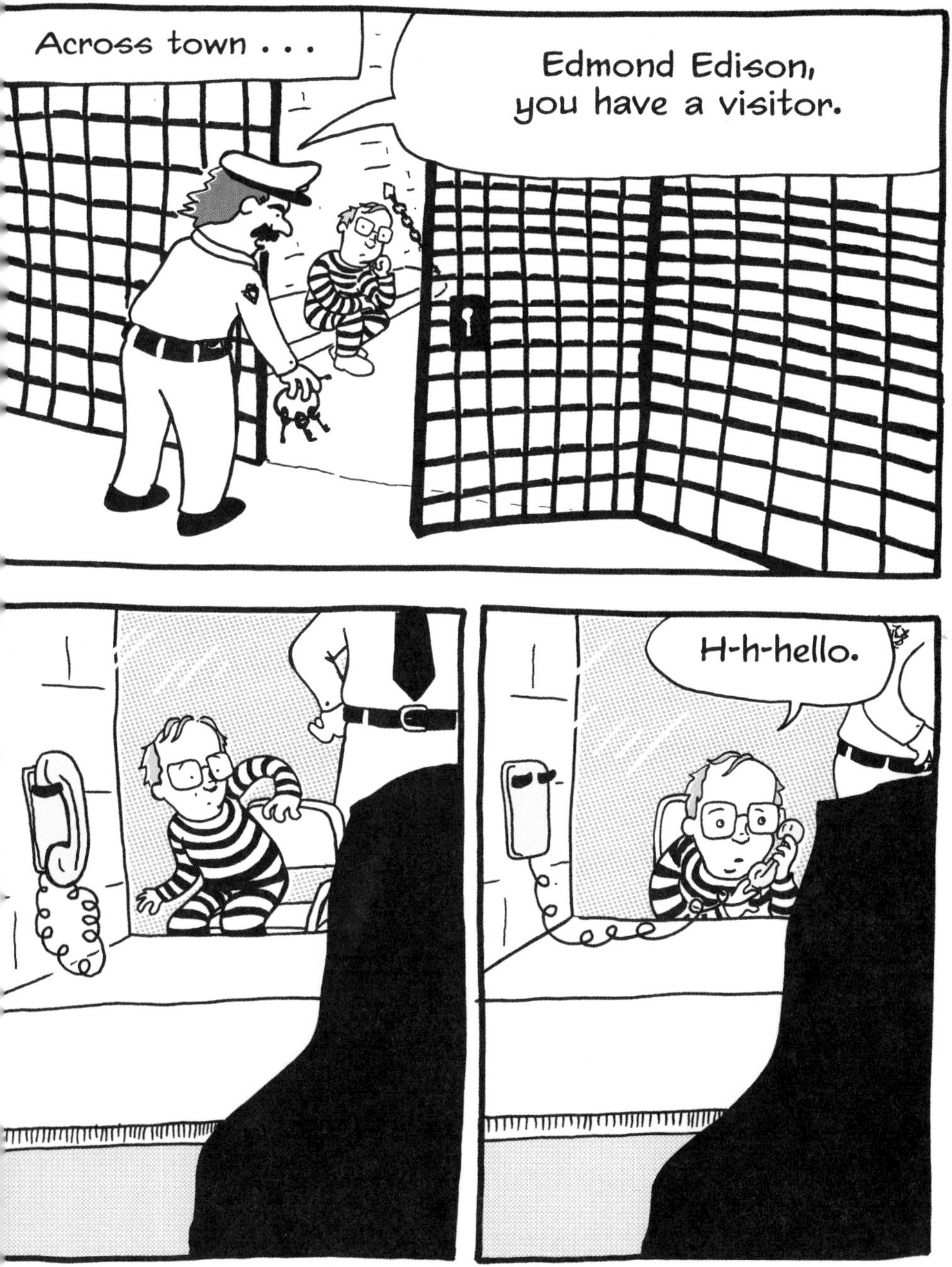
Across town . . .
Edmond Edison, you have a visitor.
H-h-hello.

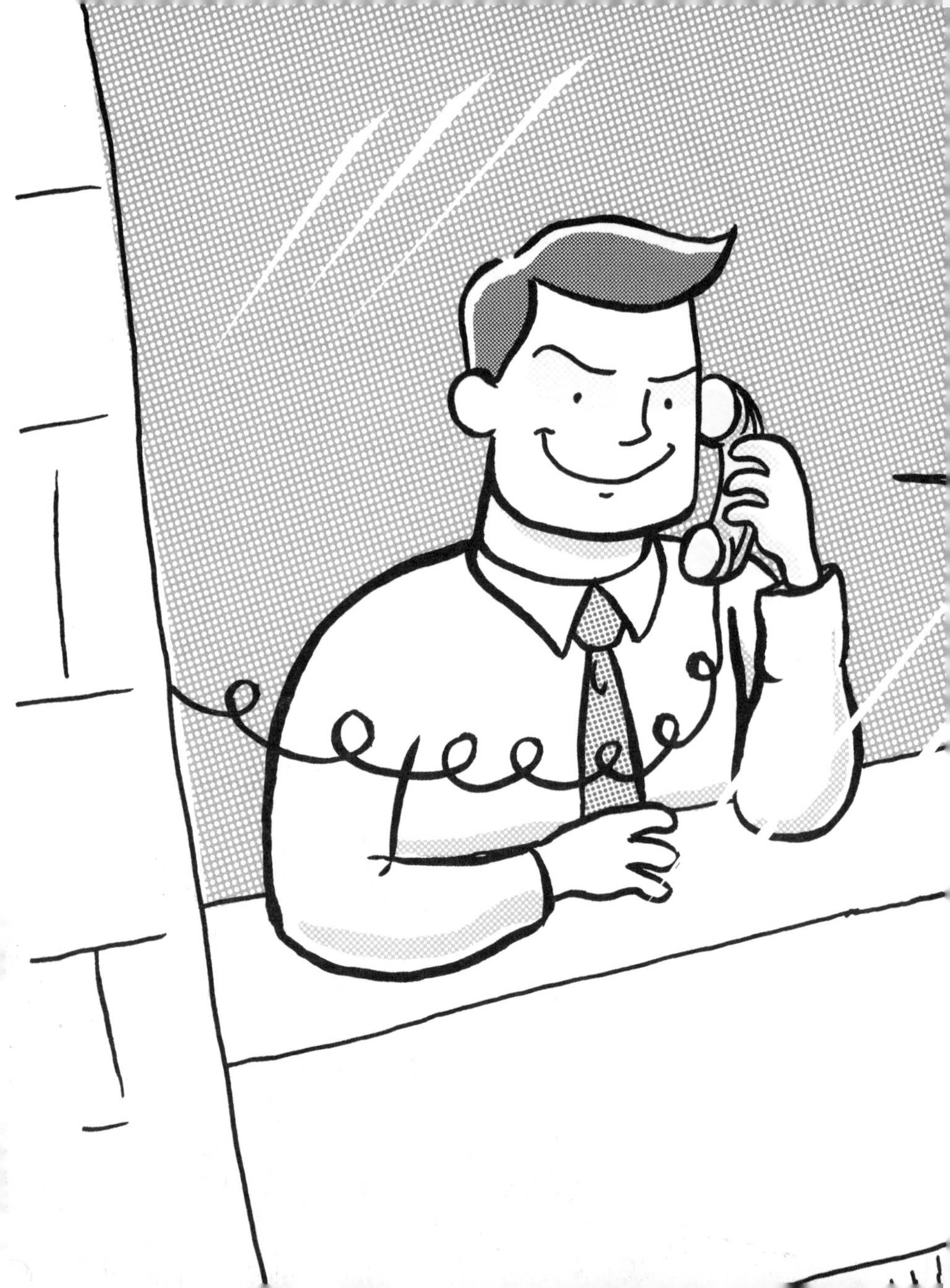

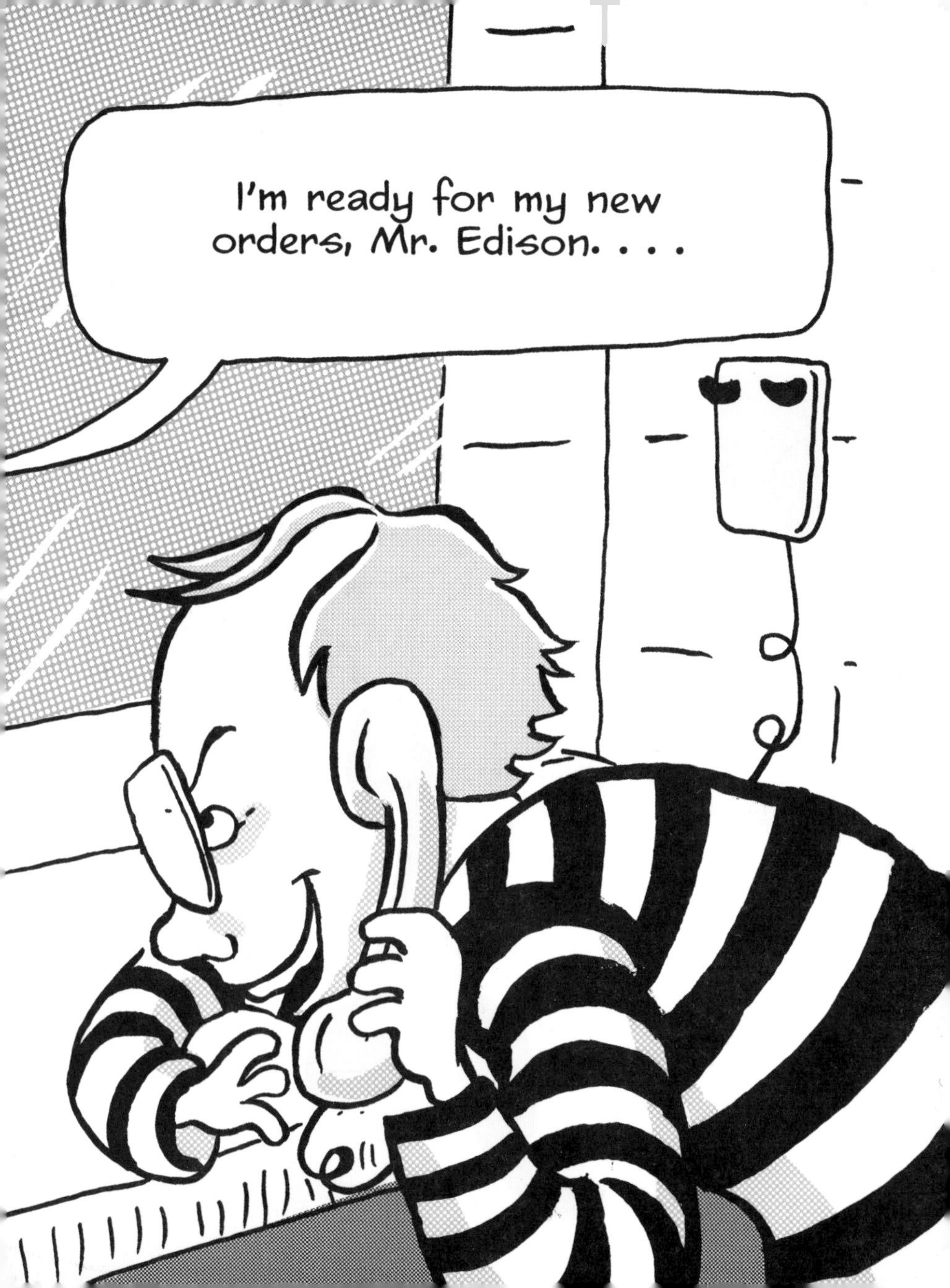
I'm ready for my new orders, Mr. Edison. . . .

FOR MY G
—J.J.K.

THIS IS A BORZOI BOOK PUBLISHED BY ALFRED A. KNOPF

Visit us on the Web! www.randomhouse.com/kids

Educators and librarians, for a variety of teaching tools,
visit us at www.randomhouse.com/teachers

Library of Congress Cataloging-in-Publication Data
Krosoczka, Jarrett.
Lunch lady and the cyborg substitute / Jarrett J. Krosoczka. — 1st ed.
p. cm.
Summary: The school lunch lady is a secret crime fighte   ll
the popular teachers wi
ISBN 978-0-375-84683-0 (trade) — ISBN
1. Graphic novels. [1. Graphic novels. 2. Robots—Fictic
Fiction. 4. Schools—Fict
PZ7.7.K75Lu 2(
[Fic]—dc22
2008004709

The illustrations in this book were created usin;

MANUFACTURED IN
July 2009
20 19 18 17 16 15

First Edition